SLEEPING DUTY

LAURA MONTGOMERY

ACKNOWLEDGEMENTS

I want to thank Barb Bernstein, Duncan Botti, Luke Botti, Kathleen F. Hodge, Autumn Killingham, Jim Montgomery, and J.M. Ney-Grimm for all their help, observations, expertise and insights. You are all pretty wonderful. Thank you.

All mistakes are solely my own.

DEDICATION

To my sons, with love, for all their help.

CHAPTER 1

DECANTING A HUMAN WAS NOT the same as decanting a bottle of wine. The doctor swore at the condition of the man and the machinery in front of him. If the word 'modern' had had any meaning for him anymore, he might have called the resuscitation chamber de-orbited from the starship long centuries ago modern, but the keep that led to it, and the cavern that housed it were anything but modern. Instead, they replicated a history of mankind long lost on its planet of origin.

Medical doctor Robert McCrary, grey, bearded, and sour, swore again, and his assistant still ignored it. Arran always ignored the swearing. He heard it a lot, and some of it was in an English that didn't match his own, but the intent was no mystery. Lord Arran McDev was not old, just twenty that winter. He had the black hair and green eyes common to the Marss, and sometimes seen amongst the Pan.

The lights in the room were bright. They were not the smoking oil lamps and candles that had lit Arran's childhood, but powered by electricity and a reactor built on another world. The room itself was of materials smoother than wood and plaster, and far cleaner than the most well kept kitchens.

Arran watched all the steps the doctor took, making sure to test him against the checklist. Arran had copied that checklist out longhand many times in the five years he had studied with the ship's doctor. He would be in charge of the checklist one day, and he could repeat it by heart. Much of it, he even understood, because someone had to be able to keep the resuscitation chamber running on its generator, fix the cryogenics, and maintain the nutrients for all the frozen sleepers from the starship.

If he understood more, he might become a physician like Dr. McCrary. If only he and the doctor were allowed to wake all the sleepers they would have a veritable university from which to learn.

Arran was not sure whether this sleeper would be useful in an academic sense or have any understanding of science. Soldiers, in Arran's experience, were not interested in such things. Usually, the Marss woke useful men—builders, architects, engineers, and medical doctors. This time, with the threat of the Pan, the king wanted a soldier. The king said he wanted someone who understood tactics, someone who had earned the right to be awakened—as so few of his kind were—and who could defend them against the depredations of the horned Pan.

King Clarence was a young man and sought a young man's sleeper. The king had taken Arran aside shortly before sending him back here with the message for the doctor. Clarence spoke very seriously about how he wanted someone both brave and learned, someone who could share the secrets of their past, of Earth, and inspire the people for the hard war ahead. The fiftieth year, the year of an awakening, had fallen to his reign, and, since his father's sleeper doctor mercifully still lived despite his age, Clarence could expand the skills available.

It was hard to say what the fellow looked like through the lid of his casket. Even setting aside the distortions of the glass, he appeared a wasted, emaciated shell, not lovely to look at, not lively with glow, not anything.

His bones were fine, with a long straight nose, and the kind of square jaw the women loved, but the sleeper was just a sketch of a person, and no more. Arran had trouble shaking the conviction the man was dead, but the doctor had been like this once, although Arran had not been born when Robert McCrary awoke filled with wrath.

The wrath was long gone, leaving only stories and the swearing.

Dr. McCrary entered the final codes to open the lid. Arran's stomach clenched, and he held his breath. It was not involuntary. The doctor had opened the lid on a different casket three days before, and the smell had given them all the information they needed. That sleeper had received a proper burial, and Dr. McCrary had drunk himself into a stupor that lasted for two days. They were only here now because Arran had given orders to remove the wine from the physician's reach.

"Cell's a go," Dr. McCrary said. He didn't call the sleeper's enclosure a casket. He said it was demoralizing.

Arran checked all the settings, particularly on the nutrients and the gasses. He nodded.

The casket—the cell—hummed in a minor key, and the upper lid separated from the portion that housed the machines that kept the body and brain alive. The smallest of sounds, a pop like lips separating at speed, accompanied the breaking of the seal, and cool airs, mercifully free of aroma, left the quarters with a metallic sigh. The casket was not metal, but a carbon of the lightest weight.

Arran would not have minded armor of that material, not that he needed it as a physician's assistant and scientist. He could handle a sword because his father had made certain all of his sons could, but Arran was no soldier.

The lid moved slowly back on its own, neither flung

nor dropped as it would have been had human hands performed the task, and Arran glimpsed a man who could claim centuries to his age. He might not have been awake for most of them, but before he slept this soldier had seen other worlds, other suns, travelled between the stars before coming to this world to settle and build a new life. But instead of doing so on the timetable the soldier expected, his comrades had left him in cold storage, part of a living library for the settlers and their descendants, a connection to Earth and other humans in the event Earth ever discovered this lost world. It had seemed like a good idea at the time.

The sleeper had some color in his face, but the blue around his lips was not a preferred tint.

The doctor breathed out loudly through his nose. "Put this one under myself, the young fool. Gilead Tan is his name. Start the saline."

The sleeping cell was on a table some three feet off the ground, and Arran reached in easily enough to prep the man's vein for the drip. When the fluids started flowing, the two men, one young and one old, settled back to wait. It would take awhile, and Arran said, "May I start the bath?"

The other man shrugged. "Sure. But it'll take as long as it takes."

Arran knew that, but he wanted something to do, and he knew the sleeper would need to have the preservatives flushed from his system. Dr. McCrary had told him it was less painful if one slept through it, so it seemed the decent thing to do.

First, he changed out the small tanks in the bottom housing. The doctor always said that the sleeping cells were designed for a long time in star travel, but not for centuries on a humid and dirty planet. There were so many ways things could go wrong over the centuries, and the sleepers were lucky that Robert McCrary had been awakened when he was, because he had found much that needed repair. He had, no doubt, saved many suspended lives.

Next, Arran re-checked all the lines—which he had first checked the day before—against the readings they should be showing on the machinery. The machinery in this room, in the entire cavern housing the portions of the starship de-orbited so many centuries back, was still alien to Arran. He thought of looms and horse-pulled tractors as machines. These slim, carbon boxes and wands were less machine and more magic. The doctor could use them, but did not, he assured the king repeatedly, know how to fix them. This baffled the king, who would try slyly from time to time to trick the doctor into admitting to knowledge of what the doctor called computers. If the king had ever succeeded, Arran had not heard of it.

By the time Arran had started the bath that would flush Gilead Tan's veins, the sleeper's color had improved more. It was hard to say that his skin had improved. Now, although it no longer looked like paper, it strongly resembled the texture of a hard cheese, as if it could crack if the man so much as blinked.

Without looking up, Arran asked, "Should we tell him to keep his eyes closed?"

"No need yet," the older man said. He gestured to a monitor. "He's still sleeping. Or brain-dead." He said the last in a mumble, but like so many old men spoke louder than he knew.

"Is that a risk still?" Arran asked.

"It was always a risk," McCrary said. "More than three centuries later? It's really a risk."

They could have left. They both knew the process could take hours, but they stayed and watched the readouts, checked the tanks, and watched the slow drip. Arran found himself staring into space, having imaginary conversations with the man, or better yet a different sleeper who wasn't a soldier. An engineer would have been nice.

The blue left Gilead Tan's lips, and he looked less like a block of cheese and more like someone with human skin. His nails and dark hair were short, which spoke volumes about his state of suspended animation. There was no animation in the sleeping cell, not even as much as possessed a corpse.

Suddenly, a tremor ran through the body, and Arran almost jumped. Robert McCrary just nodded, as if he were used to the signal. Gilead Tan's chest convulsed, and he took a long, shuddering breath. He began to breath evenly, like a sleeping child. His eyeballs shifted behind the lids, oscillating rapidly. The doctor grunted. "That's all good."

Arran let out his breath, as if he'd stopped breathing when the sleeper started. He looked at the doctor and smiled. "You were a sleeper once," he said.

Dr. McCrary grunted again. "Don't I know it? Look." He pointed with his chin.

The sleeper's mouth was working and he swallowed, his Adam's apple moving. It might have been his imagination, but Arran thought a small smile moved on the sleeper's lips.

His eyes opened. They were brown and very pale, and tracked wildly between the two men. "Hi," he said, his voice raw and cracked. "Is Andrea up yet?"

Gilead looked at the two men. One looked somewhat familiar and wore regular clothes, but Gilead couldn't place him. The other man was younger than Gilead's twenty-five years, somewhere around twenty perhaps, and dressed as if for the theater. He wore a loose-sleeved, loose-necked shirt in white, and tight, fitted breeches. Maybe it was talk-like-a-pirate day and the youth had gotten carried away. He even carried a pair of short, beveled sticks with handles at the ends slung from a loop at his belt, as if the sticks were a couple swords. He was white, dark-haired, green-eyed, lean faced and long limbed. If he'd been wearing proper clothes he would have looked like an academic or a banker, neither of whom Gilead liked as a general rule.

His reconnaissance of the more likely threat complete, he took stock of the other. The older man was grey, and had allowed his face to grow a beard, which Gilead rarely saw. He supposed that if you moved to a settler's world, you could get a little weird and no one would mind. He brought his hand to his own face. The hand trembled weakly, but he was relieved to find his face clean-shaven and still depilated. He was weak, but he'd been through this before, and knew it was important to move around. He tried to bring his elbows under him.

It didn't work. He sighed. He had always known this stuff wasn't perfect. He'd heard stories, but decided against remembering the worst ones. "Guys? I'm a little rusty. You don't have any bad news for me, do you?"

They stared at him for long seconds, as if perhaps they had just that. Finally, the older one spoke. "I hope not, but don't know yet. May I?"

He took Gilead's hand and worked it, testing the joints in all directions. "It was like this for me," the man said, "but now I'm fine."

Gilead figured the man for a doctor from the settler's portion of the ship. He didn't know they brought such old people along. Everything he'd read said there was an age limit. "You're kind of older than me, doc."

The man tilted his head and smiled, continuing his ministrations on Gilead's arm. "You don't recognize me, do you?"

Gilead felt slightly embarrassed. He'd thought the doctor looked familiar. "Sorry. You look familiar, but I don't remember you." He wasn't sure he'd met anyone that old since leaving Earth at eighteen to join the service.

He wasn't in the service anymore. It was a sweet deal, this one. He and Andrea had met in boot camp, and both survived their seven years subjective. If the military certified you weren't a psychopath, some of the colony ships would hire former service members. You'd serve the colony another seven years, either in defense or as police, and get your plot of land when you mustered out. He and Andrea had searched hard, and been really lucky to land a spot on the *Valerie Hall* bound for New Mars, which had only recently been terraformed, but long enough that higher mammals roamed free and lived, the kudzu thrived, and other people had built the first houses.

Soon they would be off the ship. They told you you couldn't hear the civilian settlement ships, and he finally believed it true. What was strange was that he would have sworn he couldn't feel it either. Maybe he was paralyzed. He really didn't want to think about that. "What's it like?" he asked.

The old man looked away. "What's what like?" he muttered.

"New Mars. Has anyone been down yet?"

"We didn't go there," the doctor said. "There was a problem. You won't recognize the sky."

Damn wormholes. "Can we get back?" Gilead asked.

"No," the doctor said slowly. "No, we can't get back." The young guy in the pirate shirt picked up his other hand and followed the doctor in kneading it. He stared fixedly at the hand.

"Have we found a new place?" They were so damned serious. Either he was paralyzed, they were all going to die, or they were under attack.

The guy in the pirate shirt looked cheerful for the first time, which was a relief, but the doctor spoke over the kid as he opened his mouth, saying, "We have, lad. It's very habitable."

That was all Gilead needed, and he returned to his first focus. "And Andrea Fielding? She's not up yet?" If she had been, she would have been at his side right now. He would be at hers.

Again the doctor spoke. "No. No, she's not up. You need to rest. Your muscles need a course of stimulation before you can use them, it looks like, so close your eyes."

He closed his eyes, but they sprang open again immediately. "Was this a combat wake that left me like this?" A combat wake would have—should have—had him on his feet in less than ten minutes. He and Andrea had volunteered for it to get a discount on their tickets. It meant they would be awakened in defense of the ship, but that was seldom needed.

"No," the doctor assured him.

The doctor and pirate-boy had taken the slower more deliberate approach with a full flush. Gilead wondered how bad a sign it was that he felt like this after what was supposed to be a less jolting wake.

As if noting the concern in Gilead's face, the doctor said, "I'm not surprised this isn't easy. Now, close your eyes."

Gilead closed his eyes and kept them closed this time. He wanted to be strong enough to walk by the time Andrea awoke. He was glad they had gotten him first. If one of them had to be weak, he didn't want it to be him, and he could probably get his strength back soon. He flexed his fingers, and the action filled him with joy. He would recover, and he and his new wife had an entire habitable planet ahead of them. He couldn't wait to see it.

CHAPTER 2

THE NEXT TIME GILEAD WOKE, he sat up. He had to hand it to them; the machines knew how to take care of a body. Whatever they put in you to keep you out and preserved was flushed from his system, and he was starting to feel normal, if not very strong. That would change. The military only gave the enhancements to those who were strong enough to handle them, and Gilead had been born, unenhanced, a natural athlete. When he got his gear back, he would make sure all of him was in working order, but he preferred, in the normal way of things, to restore himself before rebooting the extras. They made him hungry all the time, for one thing.

He was hungry now, in fact, and he smelled something that made his dry mouth start to water. Someone had put clothes on him, a pair of loose fitting pants held with a drawstring, and a long smock. They were comfortable enough, although the pants stopped halfway down his shins.

He was able to move his feet, and he felt around for his kit automatically, like he had so many times before but his toes didn't reach it. It held all his vitals, his comm, his hand weapon, and a small toolkit. The comm had his wedding pictures.

"There is soup," someone said. "And some eggs." It was the same dark-haired young man who had been in the room with the doctor when Gilead awoke the first time. His green eyes shone as if Gilead were a really exciting specimen of some sort.

There was a bowl and a small porcelain dish on one of the tables in the lab.

"It smells amazing," Gilead said. It did. If he hadn't known better, he would have sworn that the aroma drifting toward him was of real meat, chicken even.

The assistant came over. He was still in his pirate shirt and vest, and if it wasn't Halloween, Gilead had to worry about him. "My name is Arran McDev," the other said. "May I help you up?" His accent was strange, and Gilead wondered what part of Earth or Mars he had come from.

Gilead waved him off. "Let's see what I can do on my own." He had his feet planted firmly on the floor, and slowly pushed up through them. Like hell he was going to fall. From heels, ankles and slightly wobbly knees, everything worked up through his hips. Now for a step.

That worked, too, and with a great effort of will he took a step without falling over, even though his body felt as if it wanted to. He took another step, and despite the fluidity of his knees and all the bones in his legs, he found himself able to walk toward the table. "I'll tell you, Arran," he said, "I was a little worried earlier when I couldn't move at all. This is better."

He reached the table, and found himself happy to grip the back of the chair. He noticed it for the first time. Unlike every other chair he had ever seen on a spacecraft, it neither grew out of the floor nor was bolted down. He was pretty sure it was made of wood. He looked up with puzzled eyes, but the other seemed to notice nothing strange.

The soup—he was here for the soup. Once he had seated himself and started eating, he struggled to control the desire to lift the bowl and gulp it down.

Fortunately, it was too hot. There was little in it besides stock, but even the reconstituted potato was strangely delicious. He figured that was because it was his first meal after a long sleep. The scrambled eggs were equally delicious.

Arran hovered the whole time he was eating, but Gilead ignored him. When he was finished, he wiped his mouth, carefully placed his hands on the table edge—just in case—and pushed himself up. He was fine.

As if he had been watching, the doctor returned when Gilead finished.

As Gilead slowly walked around the room, the doctor explained that they would put him on an exercise regimen, and give him lots of food, which was a relief. Sometimes pickings were lean at the end of a long voyage. Maybe the ship had lost its way early in the trip and found the new planet immediately. That had been a stroke of luck.

The doc covered a lot of biology while discussing his plans for Gilead's recovery, and Gilead, feeling the surge of strength the food brought on, finally interrupted to ask after the others. Six soldiers from Gilead and Andrea's old unit had signed for this voyage. The six had served together a long time, interviewed well with the company, and the military had certified them clean of mental anomalies. That was sometimes a question, but screening at the end of service could identify most bad ticks. All told, the security personnel totaled over twenty persons, but he and his wife had only known the rest for the length of their training period.

"About that," the doctor said. "How about you take a seat?"

Since the doctor had taken the wooden chair for himself, Gilead returned to the sleeping cell and sat on the edge. He looked forward to a real bed.

Arran stood with arms folded near the doctor,

looking grim enough to be a real pirate. The older man slumped in his chair, wiping a hand across his mouth and beard. "Some very strange things have happened since you signed on."

Something in the back of Gilead's brain must have been putting together the odd signs—the shirt, the chair, the lack of vibration—for he found himself feeling preternaturally calm, upright but relaxed, ready to run or fight. It was an old feeling, but not one he usually experienced in a doctor's room. "Tell me," he said softly, and received a sharp look from Arran, who stopped leaning against the wall.

"For starters," the doctor said, "we're on the ground."

Going by bone-feel, this was no surprise, but the presence on the ground of the ship's lab was. He recognized it from when he went under the cold sleep. He studied the doctor again, more closely this time. He knew now why he recognized him—this was the guy who'd checked him out before the cold sleep. He said nothing of that. "The ship is on the ground?" The manufacturers constructed even interplanetary spacecraft on orbit, never mind a real interstellar starship. It wasn't like they could land.

McCrary had not been fooled. "You recognize me now?"

"You're older," Gilead said slowly. A lot older. The man's subjective time was clearly different than his own. "Were we lost for a long time?"

"The ship got here a long time ago," Arran said in his strange accent. "More than three hundred years ago."

Jesus, that was as long as the time between the first man landing on the moon and the discovery of how to use wormholes. That was one of those units of time they taught you to measure your own subjective against, even though he was born long after the wormholes became useful, and he knew nothing of the time when man first got off Earth. He looked at the doctor, and blurted the first stupid thing that popped into his head, "You're three hundred years old?"

McCrary snorted. Arran scowled.

Gilead looked at both of them. "And you're just now waking us up?"

"Just you," McCrary said. "I've only been up for fifty years myself."

"Those are the rules," Arran supplied unhelpfully.

But Gilead focused on only one thing. "What do you mean, 'just me'? What about the others?" He was standing now. He looked at the door. It had become a lot more interesting now that he knew it didn't lead to a sterile corridor in an orbiting starship.

"They stay sleeping," Arran said grimly. "It is not their time."

"I want my wife," Gilead said. He felt relaxed physically, and mentally wary.

"We cannot wake her," Arran went on. "We may only wake one of you every fifty years. You are the one for us. The king wanted a soldier."

"You have a king?" Gilead asked. He studied the two of them. He knew what a king was, some sort of inheritable dictatorship. It was clear that things had gone very poorly on this planet. "Is he the guy with this fifty year rule?"

"We all have the rule," Arran said. "The Marss have the sleepers and we follow the traditions set down long ago."

"By your ancestors?" Gilead asked. The door was not far. He did the breathing pattern that booted up a certain enhancement. He felt pretty good. He tried to recall the layout of the labs. He and Andrea had walked by the honeycomb where they kept you in your sleeping cell. If they had kept the layout, it should be to his left when he exited the room. Might not be, but you had to make a call if you were going to move fast.

Arran nodded. "Yes. By our ancestors."

"I had a contract with those ancestors of yours," Gilead said. The door didn't have any kind of palm pad that he could see. A mental image presented itself, a memory of the young woman who had escorted Andrea and him swiping the swirly spot in the door. The ship had been so very new and had had all the latest tech. Going by the wooden chair, it was maybe still the latest tech.

"I said the same thing, son," McCrary said. "The word of the king is law around here."

"That," Gilead said, in as reasonable a tone as he could muster, considering, "is bull."

He leapt for the door. They made no move to stop him, and the swipe on the swirly thing worked just fine and he was out, surprising two men standing guard.

They had figured on his reaction, it looked like. Well, they'd been through it before with all their sleeping slaves. The gravity wasn't Earth normal, maybe a little heavier, but he was full of hot soup, scrambled egg, and adrenaline, and he could do anything.

The two men were roughly his height, the blond one maybe a little taller. They tried to be gentle with him at first, him being an invalid. The blond enveloped him in a hug, like he was a human strait jacket, but Gilead puffed and hulked up, slid out of the looseness he'd created, and from his crouch on the floor jammed his bare foot into what turned out to be an armored shin, something rough studded with metal.

Three centuries of cold sleep left a body with no calluses, but Gilead ignored the pain to his tender skin, revised the trajectory of his foot, and shot it upward. The blond bellowed, clutching his groin, but somehow managing to raise his own booted foot as if he'd squash Gilead like a bug.

It was time to roll, so Gilead did, and he was on his feet, the maimed blond between him, and the other fellow, unfortunately, and the corridor to the left.

Even a lightning quick inspection in that direction showed, however, that his memory of the ship's layout was not worth the aged brain cells that held it. A corridor of stone stretched into the distance, and showed no other doors like the one through which he had come. One direction was as good as another, so he went right, away from the hostile natives.

He had always been fleet of foot, and he ran like a gazelle, the centuries of cold sleep having no effect on him. He was the wind coursing through these halls of stone, past small, recessed nooks in the walls, but never a window. The nooks held what looked to be oil lanterns, the source of the smoke he had smelled earlier, but his passage did not stir them.

Still he was the wind.

There was light of a different quality up ahead. He wasn't sure he knew how to recognize daylight in this place, but it seemed golden, as if there were a functioning sun; but there was also something else, almost blue and almost green, but really neither. Who knew the nature of the light this planet's star shed?

The air also smelled different. He heard shouts behind him, and his lips pulled back in a feral grin. He did not have a complete plan, but he knew he needed to gain his freedom if he wanted to get Andrea and the others out. He might have to kidnap the doc or his helper, but he could read and he'd watched several resuscitations before. He'd practice on someone he didn't know first, maybe a Marss.

He slowed and stopped. He had reached the end of the hall. It opened to a set of stairs ascending. No video of haunted castles he had ever seen matched the cold drear of those steps. Large slabs of mortared stone, cut to a uniform tread, curved round a central pillar. There was a window overhead. More important, on the other side of the stairs stood an open doorway.

He eeled around the stairs, almost losing his footing on a wet spot, and stopped again. He stood in an opening in the side of a mountain, a low balustrade the only barrier between him and a rocky drop below. The sun was yellow, as sun for the children of Earth.

The rock face fell away maybe five hundred meters to a creek bed filled with rock and boulders. The other side of the creek flowed into grasses of aquamarine and yellow green. The grass was also filled with boulders. There were no trees for cover. The incline of the rock face was a little short of ninety degrees. They wouldn't expect him to try it, but he could handle it easily.

Lichen grew on the balcony. It would have been lichen, if it weren't the blue they called indigo. It gave off a scent when the cool wind blew through, and the smell was clean and soapy. If he'd been on Earth, he would have called it springtime, but the angle of the sun was subtly off in the deep cobalt above, in a way he couldn't quantify, but that some part of him understood. He was on another alien world, and he was fighting someone again.

Here, as on Earth, it seemed that no matter the height, the plant life scored the rock and burrowed in. A small, scrappy shoot of something brown with bark grew out of the rock face. He reached for it.

His survey had only lasted a second, but the angry voices were closer and he swung himself off the little balcony onto the stunted growing thing, which might or might not have been a tree or at least might have wanted to be a tree if it weren't growing out of an almost vertical rock face.

It passed his test. It held him. Barefoot, it was easy to find the invisible footholds, the small declivities which he could trust with his weight, but only because he was crazy. He had the training, he knew how to do this, and he began to move.

A voice sounded. It was Arran, one of his captors. He sounded worried. "Get back here, you fool. You'll fall and die."

The young man wasn't necessarily wrong, but Gilead had calculated the risk very quickly. If asked, he would have said it was obvious. He would do Andrea and his comrades no good as a captive. Therefore, he had to leave. Who knew how he would get back in and revive them, but staying put didn't offer him much in the way of choices. It was likely they would have locked any door on him.

Now, if they caught him, it was guaranteed. He had covered maybe a dozen meters, and counted on the fact that they wanted him alive. They shouldn't shoot him, and it didn't look like they had guns. For all he knew, they had arrows. His back prickled, but he ignored it. There was nothing he could do and he had made his calculations and his choices.

The yelling didn't last long. He didn't waste an upward look at the balcony, but he figured they were trying to race him to the bottom. His hurried look had shown no doors in the rock below, but a recessed one might not show.

His left hand slipped. He found another point to hold, and paused for a moment to rest. He right foot was on an actual ledge, which was a luxury he could use at that moment. He didn't rest long. He couldn't afford to. He resumed his descent.

They were waiting at the bottom.

There were more of them this time.

Two had ropes, and one had a net. The blond one

was just large, and he and Gilead had already made contact earlier. Arran stood back of them with his arms folded, clearly not planning to participate in the attempted capture. The old man had not joined them.

Gilead started a crabbed, sideways glide, angling up. He would leave them behind, find another entrance before the manic power deserted him.

Gilead caught the first lasso, and stopped it from settling around him. Since he couldn't wrest the line away, he slipped the noose over a jutting rock just to slow things down.

The second followed too close on the first and yanked him off the rock face. He landed in a crouch, but they had a net waiting for him, and someone flung it like a heavy cloud and sealed him in. He stopped struggling as soon as he realized it was doing him no good, but his captors did not return the favor. He lost consciousness when the angry one took his revenge with a kick to the head.

When Gilead awoke, he was alone. The bed was comfortable enough, but he was not back in the resuscitation lab. There were no electric lights, just a pair of the little gas lamps, only one of which burned with a clear white flame, and a barred window at shoulder height.

When he sat up, his head throbbed. He gingerly probed the lumps with his fingers, and decided there was no permanent damage. His hand came away sticky, and he looked for a faucet. He saw none, just a basin and a pitcher. He sighed.

His choices had been reduced. He would have to go with what he had. His instinct to get the hell out had been a good one, but, trapped, he might have the chance to learn more. He had had instructors and mates in his unit who would have pointed out that it was his own actions that had reduced his choices, but his mates had always been grateful enough when his quick decisions were good ones.

He prowled the room, waiting for the throbbing in his head to subside. He knew it would, soon enough. It always did.

In addition to the bed, the room held a table with two small chairs, a rug that cut the chill of the stone on his bare feet, and a small table that held the water pitcher and basin, and below that, what he finally figured might be a chamber pot. He groaned, and was filled with a deep and burning desire for real plumbing.

God knew what the life expectancy was in this place. He wondered if they bathed. He hadn't noticed a particular smell on them, but perhaps that was the cold sleep. You didn't always notice you weren't on a starship, and you couldn't always smell much either. He'd read that somewhere, but maybe that was wrong. He'd smelled the lichen. Even if he didn't like the people here, he might have to concede they could be clean enough.

He eyed the oil lamp. He could set the room on fire. That would bring them running, but if he did that, they'd put him in a worse room with no light. There had already been one drop in the quality of the accommodations.

He tested the door, and found it much as it looked— large, heavy, and locked. There was a gap at the bottom, where it didn't meet the floor. When he attempted to lift it from there, he decided it hung on hinges. The round metal thing at waist height was a doorknob. It had a hole beneath it, which he knew was for a key. He looked through the keyhole, which was large but empty. In his sisters' books someone always left the key in the lock. There were ways to take advantage of that, especially with the size of the gap at the bottom of the door.

He heard footsteps, and returned to the bed, drawing the covers back over himself. The pillow was covered in blood; he felt bad about that.

He closed his eyes, listening for the sound of the key. Something scraped against old metal, hinges creaked, and he heard the door open. If it was just the doctor, he could get out.

Stop it, he told himself. *Don't do that again. It didn't work.*

Footsteps approached the bed. He was pretty sure there were two people. He heard Arran's voice, "I'll take care of his head. It likely looks worse than it is." Gilead hoped he meant that nicely.

The doctor spoke next. "I know you're awake. We have three guards at the door, including the guy you got in the nuts. He still doesn't like you."

Gilead scowled and muttered, as if the talking disturbed him. A wet cloth touched his forehead, and that did disturb him. He jerked away, and sat up.

"I'm going to clean you," Arran said patiently.

Gilead eyed the damp cloth with distrust. "Is it clean?"

Arran looked offended. "Of course, it is."

Gilead looked to the doctor for confirmation.

"They understand germ theory, son. It's not antiseptic always, but it's aseptic. They're not going to infect you."

Gilead pulled himself to the side of the bed and let Arran minister to the lump and the open cuts. The kicking man had been wearing boots.

"How did you do that?" Arran asked.

"Do what?" Gilead said. He tried not to wince. In primitive cultures, he'd read somewhere, it was important not to show pain. He was clearly in a primitive culture. The next probe was less gentle, and he gave up and swore.

"Fight. Run. Climb."

"I'm a soldier. We do all that stuff." Gilead closed his eyes and endured. Maybe they could amputate his head. It was not a suggestion he planned to make out loud.

"But right after you've been sleeping for centuries?" Arran continued his probing. "I heard that Dr. McCrary was fatigued for weeks."

Gilead felt a reluctance to talk about what they had all seen with their own eyes. Why confirm their observations? "I don't know about the doc."

"This is why the king wants you," Arran said, as if talking to himself. "The stories are true."

"What stories?" Gilead asked, hoping to change the topic.

"About the superior abilities of the soldier race," Arran said.

"We aren't a race," Gilead demurred. He let his eyes open to slits and checked out the doctor. The old man didn't seem to be planning any big medical explanations.

"But you recover very quickly," Arran pointed out.

"We do. And," Gilead went on, inspired, "we are trained very hard on a quick wake up. We might be needed immediately."

The old doctor grunted. "Do they teach you to think things through first?"

Gilead ignored this. It was too close to what he had been thinking. He had given away a lot with his escape attempt, besides an unlocked door, and that included information about his more obvious enhancements.

The doctor wouldn't let it go. "Do they teach you to go off half-cocked? Like a big stupid? I'm not sure the king will be interested in such a poor tactician."

Despite the failure, Gilead didn't agree with the doctor's assessment. His captors had learned about him, but he had learned a lot, too, and seen the outside with his own eyes, knew he could breathe the air, and knew he could live. If he'd made it, it would have been well worth it.

"What does the king want with me?" Gilead asked.

"Arran?" the doctor said. "What does the king want with Gilead here?"

Arran was ignoring the undercurrents. Gilead couldn't tell whether Arran understood them at all. "He wants a soldier as strong as the Pan."

CHAPTER 3

T HE DOCTOR HAD LAUGHED AT Gilead about his mental state, and he supposed his failure to escape could have meant it wasn't that good. He always awoke physically capable. Maybe that long a sleep had done something to his brain. Hindsight was a great thing.

It turned out that a few centuries of cold sleep made your beard grow when you woke up. Had he not seen the doctor's excess of facial hair, he might not have realized what he was dealing with when the first stubble came in. He asked Arran for shaving equipment, which turned out to be a razor, soap, water and a basin. There was a little brush. The kid laughed at him when he asked for instructions.

He finally found a use for the mirror in his room, given how little he needed to see to brush his dark hair. His hair was still short, of a brown so dark it was almost black. He stared at its spikes in the mirror, and rubbed them down with wet hands. The heavy dark brows, the pale brown eyes, they all looked familiar and stark against his pale skin.

The bones of his face were harsh and pronounced, and even when he put his weight back on they would stand out, but he took their current prominence as a sign that he needed to get a little healthier. He covered his lower face with lather from the soap, thumbed it off his mouth, and set to shaving. It was almost a scraping, but the blade removed the stubble, and the lather and his hair floated in the basin's water. The amazing thing was that he would have to do this again tomorrow.

It was an alarming exercise, with the straight edge so close to his throat, but he didn't cut himself and was pleased enough with the results. He felt as if he had reached some small measure of civilization, or figured out how to express it himself. The pale brown eyes in the mirror approved.

When he wasn't walking his strength back, he brooded. If he had lost his mental acumen, or even just his patience, he wasn't at his peak. He wasn't sure how he'd tell if he'd gone stupid—he wouldn't be smart enough to know. The worse fear, the one he knew festered inside him but he wouldn't consciously consider, was the fear that decay was setting in with the others, with Andrea. He had to get them out.

He claimed that his manic burst had exhausted him, and let them think him weaker than he was. They wanted him to walk outside. He insisted on walking inside, claiming that the bright daylight hurt his eyes. The doctor knew he lied, but said nothing, only urging him to try a little at a time each day. He agreed to that.

In the meantime, he learned the corridors of Stampo, the fort. Some called it a castle because long ago some romantic had lost his mind and persuaded the other idiots that feudalism was a good thing. He couldn't wait to be a warrior serf. He already hated the king of the Marss.

He learned a lot in his wanderings. Aboveground, the fort formed something like an L bordering on growing into a T, with two full, two-story, southern and eastern wings. A bump to the north held a courtyard and a large entry hall. His own room, which was in an eastern corner of the eastern wing, looked out on a meadow through its northern window. Across the meadow and to the northeast lay the fabled city of First Landing, as the Marss still called it with a real absence of imagination.

To make Fort Stampo level with an alpine meadow already in place, the original builders had shorn half the top off a mountain overlooking the valley. The builders had used the shavers and tractors of Gilead's own time to hollow out a network of corridors in the rock itself. In the doctor's lab, which was inside the hollowed portion of the mountain, and in three lower levels, the seamless but sporadic plast walls served as relics of Gilead's own time, when the stuff had been poured and shaved. Gilead hadn't known plast could wear out, but the stretches of stone underneath showed him how uninformed he had been. The walls in the structure aboveground were plastless stone and far more recent.

Below ground, the structure consisted of two long corridors that met in their middles, lined with true north like a compass rose. Stairwells ran at all ends except the northern, but visitors entering by the courtyard and great hall could rely on the massive central stairwell where the corridors met. The stories above ground had a courtyard and a large entrance hall at the end of the shortened northern axis. The doctor's lab and the balcony ran along the same axis two floors below and were part of the original construction.

The squirrels who had crossed interstellar space had thought it a good idea to bury their nuts, and the sleepers were housed below ground. There had probably been some notions of embedding them deep where they would not be disturbed.

Gilead was confident that the southern corridor three levels down from the ground floor held the sleepers. The universal power sign on a door on the bottom floor in the north wing convinced him he had the floor right, and was a vision that brought tears to his eyes at the beauty of it. If the plast walls wore out, the reactor on the other side of that door did not. Like a sun, it had very few moving parts. He felt no temptation to open the door, and moved back to the center stairwell when he heard footsteps. He had been alone so far, and he wanted to keep it that way.

From his conversations with the doctor and Arran, he knew that the original settlers were to blame for the current politics, but the ones in power now weren't exactly relinquishing control over their fellows. Some jackass who wanted to be a strong leader had, coincidentally, seen the need for a strong leader when the lost starship had found the habitable world. The ship held only a few thousand people, all of whom, Gilead and Andrea included, had been on their way to New Mars, a terraformed world tailored very closely to Earth-normal. The ship of sleepers would have augmented an existing colony on New Mars, not tried to start a new one. Instead, according to local historical lore, they had done their best to make do with the population they had and build a life here on Nwwwlf, which was—not Welsh—but Not What We Were Looking For.

Things had gone poorly quickly. The contingent of eight hundred Pan had abandoned the other settlers and headed off on their own. For over one hundred years the unenhanced Marss had thought them lost until they returned to conduct raids and steal human children.

Gilead interrupted one of Arran's explanations at this point. "The Pan are human, too." They were enhanced as well, but where Gilead's enhancements were provided after he passed through puberty and joined the military, which needed and could afford such things, the Pan's enhancements were provided in the womb and could be inherited.

"Not anymore," Arran said with great determination. "They are savages. We don't know what they do with our children. Some say they eat them. Others assume slavery."

"Kind of like what you've done with the sleepers?" Gilead said.

Arran refused to respond. They stood with McCrary on the small balcony from which Gilead had attempted his escape, for his daily dose of sunlight. The balcony was on what he had learned was the backside of the fort, and the rock strewn landscape below led, maybe a kilometer away, to the rise of another mountain.

He made sure to plead light fatigue after longer and longer periods each day. He had learned his way around the lovely Fort Stampo, and gained a growing certainty about where they kept the sleepers' quarters. His own kit had everything but his weapon. Someone had taken his blaster, and he wouldn't have been surprised to learn that all the soldiers' kits had been pilfered. If the weaponry from the starship was anywhere to be found, he had seen no sign of it. He was careful not to ask. It seemed likely that the original band of thugs had kept it to themselves, and, if it still worked, would be found in the palace with the king's guard. You read a lot of military history in the service. The companies selling settlement services also forced it on you, attempting to prevent exactly what had happened on Nwwwlf.

"So you're going to war with the Pan?" Gilead asked. "I can't believe there isn't room for both of you. You do have a whole damned planet."

"They are our neighbors, and Nwwwlf is a savage wilderness."

"Also," the doc said, "this valley is probably the most valuable land on the planet for humans biologically."

Arran laughed. "The Earth enzymes are strong. Centuries of biological exchange keep us healthy here. The wild chickens are everywhere—if you don't eat an egg a day, you'll grow very weak—and a man who wants to clear new ground always brings goats." Arran got all bristly at the politics and what Gilead called the slavery, but he was like some geeky kid on the nature stuff.

"So you want to take their land?" Gilead asked. Presumably, this was the land the Pan had cleared.

"They are taking our children," Arran pointed out. He looked at Gilead directly when he said this, as if that should be reason enough. Perhaps it was, but it seemed unlikely.

"Have they taken some child of the king's?" he asked.

"No."

"How about the aristocracy?" Gilead pressed.

"No," Arran said, his irritation obvious.

"So the children are an excuse. I get it."

"You assume much," Arran said. "And you are insulting."

"You kept me in cold sleep for centuries. You're holding my wife and friends prisoner. Do you think you're going to get the benefit of the doubt?" He laughed, and squinted into the sunlight. Regardless of his lies, he liked it. It felt good on his skin, and there was always a soft wind to keep him cool. "What time of year is it?" he asked, changing tacks.

"Spring," Arran said. "Winter is ending, the farmers are planting, and the king is considering a summer campaign. The harvest was good last year, and he can field an army."

Later, Gilead studied the maps they provided him. They were flat and on paper, and showed no elevations. The mountain fastness in which they held the sleepers was part of a ring of mountains around a large valley tens of kilometers in diameter. He thought. He might not have read the map correctly, or understood Arran's explanation, but they did use the same terminology so he went with it.

Stampo was in the southwestern segment of the ring, and the back of it, the aboveground cap to the T, fronted west. He wondered if the Pan lived to the west, or if the fort was just the place to stash the sleepers. He had walked a little along the creek one day, but his memories of his first visit to it weren't good.

In the middle of the mountain ring, next to a large placid river that cut through the valley from northwest to southeast, in a curving, meandering path, stood the town called First Landing. He'd smiled when he heard the name, and Arran had looked offended.

First Landing was the capital. The king lived there with his court, and the land around it was held by his nobles, and farmed, Gilead noted with some disgust, by no one who was allowed to own the land. Arran was not familiar with the word serf.

The Pan came down the hills from the north to steal children. Traders claimed they had rich farmlands, mines of copper, coal, and iron ore, and towns of gifted artisans. Gilead wondered if it was even true about the kidnappings.

After the first four days, when he tired of his deceit, he announced that his eyes were now accustomed to the harsh light, which was not harsh at all, and, perhaps, on the soft side of the spectrum. He would like to go outside, he told his minders over breakfast, which they ate with him.

"Excellent," McCrary said. "Now we can see what you're made of."

"We'll get you a horse," Arran said.

"Can you ride?" McCrary asked.

"I'm sure I can," Gilead said. "It would help if you showed me video, of course." He looked meaningfully at the doctor, who knew full well that Gilead's skill set allowed him to learn very rapidly.

McCrary refused the bait, and turned to Arran. "Show him someone with excellent skills."

Arran looked doubtful. "Etienne is very skilled, but he's a terrible teacher."

"He'll do," Gilead said quickly. "Let me watch him."

"Have you skill with a sword?" Arran asked.

Gilead had no such skills. It didn't worry him. "I can learn that, too. Any energy weapons? Any guns?" Now was a natural time to ask.

"The guns are very unreliable," Arran said. "They sometimes hurt the user."

"You might call them muskets," McCrary said drily. He seemed amused, as if he were laughing at both of them. "And no one has energy weapons. We're lucky to have the electricity that kept you alive all this time."

That afternoon, Arran and McCrary escorted Gilead to the newest part of the keep in the truncated northern wing. The walls were plaster, not stone, which made the rooms brighter. Some had wood paneling, which was polished and glowing, casting a rich warmth that Gilead had not expected. Andrea would like something like that he thought. He'd get her some when he woke her.

At the end of the trek through the corridors, they reached a large hall with wooden doors far taller than a man. He had seen them in his prowlings, but someone had always discouraged him from approaching them without Arran or the doctor present. The doors seemed unnecessary, but they were impressive. Broad beams that had once been trees held up the ceiling, and two of the walls held rows of muskets, pikes, and swords, straight bladed and a little longer than a katana. It would have been vaguely ridiculous if he'd only been visiting. Knowing he would be spending the rest of his life here made the sight anything but ridiculous.

Gilead had been a soldier. He had seen combat, fought in two colony wars over the course of his seven years subjective, and had been injured twice. But the pikes looked so damned rusty, and he wondered if his vaccines, which were good for a lifetime, were good for three centuries.

Five long tables, able to seat twenty apiece, looked as if they would hold the garrison at dinnertime. He filed the information as at least indicative of the number of personnel.

The hall led into a courtyard of packed earth and what he might, if he had been feeling brave, called grass. It smelled like the zoo or a farm. Chickens wandered the ground, a pair of hounds slept in the sun, one with its hind legs twitching, and a young boy led a goat toward a building that looked much like a shed to the left. The wind stirred up a light cloud of dust, and someone sneezed. Winged creatures—birds?—circled lazily overhead.

To the left lay an entrance back the way he had come. It led to what he knew to be the kitchens. Their gardens lay beyond them.

It was the first time Gilead had seen so many women outside the kitchens. One carried a large basket of plant life, and the one talking at her carried nothing, but spoke with great animation. She looked as if she had come along on the chore only to complain. They both wore skirts below their knees, and open necked blouses with no support structure. Gilead grinned.

More to his surprise, he saw small children as well. It seemed strange they would occupy a fort.

A pair of men on a bench were cleaning their muskets. Gilead decided not to go near them, given the reliability issues.

The stables were on the far side of the courtyard, round a bend to the right and against the inside of the fort's outer wall.

Etienne, of course, turned out to be the blond who failed to look on Gilead with love. They stood in front of a stall housing a large brown animal.

"You want me to teach you to ride?" Etienne scoffed.

"No," Gilead said patiently. "I just want you to show me."

"Have you ever been on a horse? You can't ride them in a starship." He looked pleased with his understanding of Gilead's past.

"I have not," Gilead admitted.

"I'll tell you," Etienne said confidingly, "you have to ask them to hold very still. You stand in back of 'em, hold the tail, and climb up it. Got that?"

Although Gilead had never been on a horse, he was from Earth, and understood full well that one did not mount the animals in that fashion. "I'm not sure I get what you're saying. Why don't you show me?"

Etienne slapped him on the back, and laughed. It was a big slap, but Gilead checked himself from responding.

A stable boy brought the animal out, and proceeded to saddle it. It moved around a lot, and bared its teeth when the boy put the bridle over its ears. The boy seemed used to this, and used the opportunity to slip the bridle between its teeth. The horse rolled its eyes and looked crazed.

"Will you be riding him after me?" Etienne asked. His grin was large.

Gilead studied the animal. He looked Etienne over. Anything Etienne could do, Gilead could. "Sure. Don't go getting him all tired."

Etienne laughed, and the wind forced his long,

straight hair both up and back, and he looked a little crazed, too.

They followed the stable boy and the horse outside the walls to a large alpine meadow that rolled away gently from them. Beyond it lay the valley, and Gilead convinced himself that the speck in the distance to the northeast had to be First Landing. The air was filled with a sweet smell of flowers and honey, or the local equivalents, and Gilead told himself it wasn't such a bad place, after all. If only Andrea were awake, too. He felt the same outrage that his other companions were held against their wills, but the thought of Andrea possibly dying or dead filed him with horror.

Suddenly, the air sparkled less.

He needed to focus. With false patience, Etienne briefed him on how to hold the stirrup leather, where to put his foot, and how to get from the ground to the back of the horse. None of it involved clambering up the horse's tail.

Gilead watched as Etienne collected the reins, and the pair of them strode off to the left. The big man held the reins one-handed, as if he might need the other hand free for a weapon. Gilead checked what he watched against all the cine from his long-distant childhood. That this was real gave what he saw extra points for credibility, but Gilead's was not a trusting nature. The match with his memory was close enough that he figured the differences to be stylistic.

The ball of the foot rode the stirrup iron. The heels were low and pushed out. Etienne's inner calves, thighs, and butt were seamless with the horse. His back was straight, and his hands were low. He used his seat to push the horse from a walk to a trot, and Gilead thought he heard a voice command. He'd need to get those, and wondered if they were uniform across all horse systems.

The pace changed to a smoother running stride as the pair turned to arc around the field—rather than going over the end of it—and head back. "That's a canter," Arran said. He could be instructive, too.

Etienne picked up the pace again, using his hands and seat. His lips moved as well, and it frustrated Gilead that he had not made out the final word. He didn't think Etienne would share those secrets willingly.

"That's a gallop," Arran said. He stood serenely, his hands clasped loosely behind his back, like one of the instructors in boot camp. The wind picked up his hair, making him look like a young, green-eyed devil, and a small smile played about his mouth.

It was definitely a gallop, and Etienne and the horse had angled again, this time to return to their starting point on the straightest path available. It was an interesting sensation. The animal was nowhere near as fast as any vehicle Gilead had ever been in, with the exception perhaps of his old bicycle, but the mass, the sheer kinetic energy of what looked to be a combined system of maybe a 1000 kilograms took his breath away, in part because it was heading straight at him.

He assumed Etienne was pulling this stunt deliberately and knew how to stop. Arran must not have shared Gilead's assumption, for, just as the beast was about to crash through them, Arran stepped in front of Gilead, and he and Etienne both said, "Stop," at the same time. The horse stopped, its haunches dropping slightly to shed the speed. Arran took the reins.

Etienne was off the horse in a flash and stood towering over Gilead. The big blond man was only a few centimeters taller, but the proximity made him seem taller.

Gilead looked Etienne in the eyes. "Lucky Arran was able to stop it for you," Gilead said.

Etienne flushed, but, as they stood nose to nose, he started to grin. "Very lucky," he finally agreed. He stepped back and bowed. "Your turn," Etienne said.

Arran handed Gilead the reins, which were, for no reason he could tell, no longer above the creature's neck but dangling from the bit in the horse's mouth. He could ask for assistance, but it was a matter of pride to him that he need only watch something once. With all the bowing, he had missed the transition on this part of the system.

He studied the reins and the bit for what felt like far too long, took them and flipped them back over the horse's face. It worked. The rest he had seen, and, pulling the far rein away from his side of the horse, he put a foot in the stirrup, the hand with the reins on the front of the saddle, the other hand on the back, and flowed up smoothly. He settled in, situating all of himself as he had seen Etienne do. That worked, too. The beast held still, and he grinned down triumphantly.

Neither looked impressed. To them it was second nature, and, to be honest, all he was doing was sitting there.

"You have to make him move," Arran pointed out.

Etienne smirked and leaned forward. He whispered in the animal's ear, and the beast took off like a shot. In part, Gilead had been born the way he was, and not through any geneering. He had been on all the teams in school. He had worked like a dog to be good, but he had always known how to make his body learn. There was a trophy shelf in his parent's house filled with Gilead's awards. The military had provided its enhancements, but the additional training on learning had stood him in good stead before, and did so now.

He was almost grateful for Etienne's mischief. It allowed him to show what he could do. He did not say, "Stop." He settled into the saddle and rode out the gallop, commanding with his knees the curve necessary to avoid the cliff edge. He didn't want to count on the horse knowing it was there.

On the way back, he slowed to a canter, which turned out to be a smooth and pleasant gait. He tried a trot, but it was too bouncy, and he suspected he was overdoing the rising that went with it. He'd be damned if he'd walk back, and pushed for more speed. It worked. Horses were smarter than he had realized, or this one was well trained.

He needed another test. He looked around and saw a trimmed log, maybe a meter off the ground, stretched across a pair of stumps. Its use was obvious. Off to his audience's left, it provided Gilead and his mount a nice long, lead up, and he took it, setting the animal at the obstacle.

He had watched the jumping events on the Olympics once or twice. It was enough. He collected the reins and let his hands soften, leaned forward, and let the beast carry him high into the mountain air. It was very terrestrial, but exhilarating. They landed, and he didn't fall off.

He circled back to the other two, a large, foolish grin plastered across his face. "Got it," he called to them. "What else?"

"You've ridden before," Etienne said.

Gilead shook his head. "I've watched a lot of it on video. And I really paid attention to you today."

Arran was studying Gilead as if he were actually interesting. "Dr. McCrary is a terrible rider. You—you looked just like Etienne." He paused as if replaying the words in his head. "Exactly like Etienne."

Gilead dismounted, casually flipping the reins back over the horse's head. "Etienne rode real pretty. He was worth copying. Weren't you, big fella?" He slapped Etienne on the back, hard.

Etienne affected not to notice, but Gilead knew he'd jarred bone. He had his slaps finely calibrated, and this one suited a man of Etienne's size.

"What else have you got?" he asked Arran.

The kid gave Gilead the kind of considering look more common to a man twenty years older, and smiled. "Would you like to watch the sword practice?" Arran asked silkily, and his green eyes were amused. Gilead was watching his targets, but Arran was watching Gilead.

In addition to training his new skills, Gilead spent long hours in McCrary's lab reading.

It was quiet there, and he was able to debate the extent to which he let others see what he could do. The king had wanted a soldier awakened for a reason, and Gilead understood the value of demonstrating that reason to the other men. None of the women were armed as the guards were, and he figured that, with the state of technology, it wasn't surprising. Unless they wanted to remain virgins and childless their whole lives, training to fight in weapons that required muscle power was not something that most of them could accomplish with any utility. He tried to picture Andrea without her weapons, and couldn't.

Thoughts of Andrea brought their usual pang, but he had developed a plan for that issue. He was working on the first step, volunteering to help the doctor and Arran, because, he explained, he liked working on things where he could see. Only they worked with the benefit of electric light, and then only in the labs. A faint smell of lamp oil and wood smoke clung to everyone at all times.

Once, when he was alone with McCrary in the lab,

the doctor, who Arran had allowed to start drinking again, said thickly, "I know what you are doing."

"Sir?" Gilead said blankly, looking up. He had been reading a manual on nutrients, and sat in one of the two chairs brought down from orbit. It was heavenly.

McCrary looked down at him, arms akimbo. "I told you. I know what you are doing. You want to know how to work the machinery to wake your wife up."

"Doctor," Gilead said. "I understand the system. I understand there are rules against that. I just want to make sure there are no problems. These sleepers are my friends, many of them."

"You're smarter than you seemed at first," McCrary observed.

"I'm sure I had lots of preservatives running through me," Gilead said stiffly. He was still dissatisfied with his performance when he first awoke. He should have gotten away, even if his mental functioning had not been at its best.

"I just want you to know I know what you're up to," McCrary said. He wandered over to a console of monitors for which only he had the passwords. Gilead watched him closely as he ran his fingers over buttons. The holos had stopped working long ago.

"Thank you for not bringing this to Arran's attention," Gilead said. He put his finger in the manual to keep his place. It was printed on paper, not hand copied. There were some remnants of civilization, even though he might normally have considered the remnants themselves otherwise lost in antiquity.

"Oh, Arran knows. Everyone knows you want to wake your wife up." He looked over his shoulder at Gilead to gauge his reaction.

Gilead showed no emotion, although he was unhappy. "How is that?" There were only the two of them who had heard him ask for Andrea.

"Arran's a big gossip," the doctor said confidingly, worrying at his lip with his teeth. "Huge. He gossips a whole lot. You'll see. Tell him something, and you've told the whole world—or, at least the human populated parts of it."

Gilead didn't like that. It was not good for an enemy to know one's plans. "I will have to ask him about you," he said lightly. He had nothing else to say.

"I'm a big gossip, too," the doctor said. "People ask me about you all the time. They wonder how there were horses on the starships, and why people always told them the sleepers did not know how to use a sword. You are so good at both."

Gilead considered re-opening the manual or leaving. He didn't want to alienate the doctor. He wanted to build his trust, but sometimes it was hard not to get upset. The man had sold out.

"Did you ever try to wake the others?" he heard himself asking. It was a stupid question. He shouldn't have asked it. It showed he judged the man.

McCrary laughed, but it was not a happy laugh. "Of course, I did, but there was too much history working against me."

And, yet, Gilead thought, they left him here, a physician who knew how to awaken the sleepers, un-guarded and compliant. Was Arran his minder? Did they have some sort of hold on him?

As if reading Gilead's thoughts, McCrary said, "You're wondering why they leave me here with all of you, aren't you?"

Gilead nodded, and made sure to say nothing.

The older man leaned back against the console, and his eyes drifted toward the ceiling. "The king's historian, who is not without influence, has told me that my children will suffer terribly if I do such a thing."

"You married?" Gilead asked.

"I did." He looked at Gilead, and bit his lip as if forcing a penance upon himself. "My first wife was one of those who was awakened in the landing. She did not get me resuscitated, and I try not to blame her. I can't imagine what it was like then. They must all have been very frightened." He looked away again.

"The king," Gilead said, "does he know about this threat hanging over you?" Gilead couldn't imagine that a person with so much power would not know these things. The king might have ordered the threat, but kept his distance from it to maintain his image.

"It's an attempt to hold on to their Mars and Earth heritage, you know. They didn't want to lose everything we know. They had to reinvent printing to get all the information out of the starship, and they knew they couldn't rely on books to keep the knowledge. Sometimes you need someone to explain it, especially when the context changes so drastically."

"It doesn't seem to have worked," Gilead said. He thought of the packed dirt courtyard, the constant tickle of smoke in the air, and the war with the Pan.

McCrary shrugged. "It could have been worse. It could be flint and bearskins. And, having a real person for people to know keeps the past real, not mythical."

"Is it still up there?" Gilead asked. "The starship?" He didn't think it was a path home, but one never knew. It wasn't as if he knew how to operate or navigate a starship, much less one that had gotten itself lost centuries earlier.

"No one knows. The settlement lost contact with those left on it sometime in the first twenty years."

Gilead marveled. People had stayed on the ship. He wondered why. Maybe they had disagreed with the barbaric decisions of those who made the landings. "They treat human beings as a library," he said.

"True enough."

"I'm surprised they left you in there as long as they did," Gilead said. "I'd think they'd always have wanted doctors."

"I have two colleagues sleeping their lives away," McCrary told him. "Also, there are a lot of soldiers in there. They didn't seem to see a need for them in the beginning, but the engineers have always been popular. They get awakened to build marvels. Everyone gets very angry with them for not being able to replicate what took composites and nanotech and other modern basics to achieve. My predecessor was an engineer, and the stories she told would make you weep. She wound up establishing a network of smiths who performed marvelous work, but the existing guild did its best to destroy her. It's not civilized here."

"I've noticed," Gilead said drily. He would have loved a real shower. "Too bad she didn't work on the plumbing."

McCrary laughed. "That was one of her sadder stories." He pushed himself away from the console and turned around. "Read your manual. Maybe you can use it one day."

Maybe in fifty years, Gilead thought. Perhaps he could accidentally awaken Andrea, but then he'd be as old as this guy. And maybe she wouldn't want him anymore at that point—and for sure she wouldn't if he took that long to get her out.

He desperately wanted her with him. They should have awakened together, even if it would have been to a desolate wilderness. They would have faced it together, worked it together, and had their family together. If he didn't do something, she would only see him as an old man, and that was only if he were very lucky.

McCrary fiddled with the fonts on the screen, and took an incredibly long time running his programs. Gilead had trouble focusing on his reading, and took to watching McCrary's work. With McCrary's old eyes, he had increased the fonts on the screen, and Gilead could read much of it. That was good. He transitioned into the focused absorption with which he had watched Etienne ride his horse and the swordsmen with their weapons.

He recognized some of the names on the screen. He looked at the back of the old man's head, and realized he owed someone a debt. He hadn't seen Andrea's name, but maybe she had been in the earlier part of the list before he realized what McCrary was showing him. His eyes snapped back to McCrary's console. He needed to absorb what was there. He planned to be able to use it someday.

He had it narrowed down where the sleepers were quartered, somewhere in one of the corridors off the southern wing. His eyes wandered idly around the lab, looking for some sort of portable medical scanner. Some had to have made it off the ship. He was getting stronger; he just needed to get past some doors.

CHAPTER 4

ARRAN WATCHED WITH AMAZEMENT THE progress of his patient over the course of a few short weeks. The cheese-headed skeleton had rapidly put on weight, all of it muscle. Gilead Tan was broad in the back and across the shoulders, lean in the hips, long-legged and fast, a perfect specimen of a human, with an uncanny ability to learn anything. He had lost the strange accent that one could still hear in Dr. McCrary's words, and he excelled in all manner of martial arts. Arran thought this strange, given the fact that he had not fought with a sword in his past life. The weapons of the Marss' ancestors were far superior to those used now—energy and projectile weapons that could travel vast distances with pinpoint accuracy according to the doctor. The medicine was superior, and the machinery and computers could not be replicated. Every time someone died, Dr. McCrary told Arran the dead man could have been saved under the old technology. Every time the doctor was uncomfortable, he told Arran that man had changed his environment to avoid the cold, the heat, the wet, the damp, the ice, or the blazing of the sun. Arran learned not to mention the weather in McCrary's presence.

Arran kept a journal of everything he witnessed regarding the two of them, Dr. McCrary and Gilead, for he felt it was important for others to know about their lost past. One day, he hoped, the rest of humanity would rediscover the inhabitants of Nwwwlf, and find them still civilized if not fully industrialized. The doctor blamed what he called the feudalism of their society for their lack of innovation, and had laughed at the marvelous electric lights in the palace. There were six of them, and of incredible delicacy, and Dr. McCrary had muttered something about that was what happened when you let the state prevent competition with one of its revenue sources. The mockery had been untoward.

The morning he found Gilead seated in one of the starship's chairs that Dr. McCrary reserved for himself in the resuscitation lab was a revelation. To Arran's astonishment, the soldier had a manual in his hands, and his dark head was bent over it. "You read," he blurted out.

"You have books," Gilead shot back, mimicking Arran's surprise. The pale brown eyes were sardonic in the handsome face.

Arran wondered if Gilead's looks had also been gifted to him by his military, but dismissed the thought. There couldn't be any use for good looks inside the helmets they had all worn. "Of course we do," Arran said. "We have kept much."

"There's no of course about it," Gilead replied, putting his book down with his finger between the pages as if he would pick it back up as soon as Arran left him alone. "You've lost all sorts of values my people held dear. I should become a teacher and fix the situation."

Ignoring the finger between the pages and the ludicrous assertion that a soldier could ever be a teacher, Arran sat down. "We lost all the support of Earth and the starships once we were stranded."

"That's not an excuse," Gilead said.

"For what?"

"For robbing a person of his freedom. You have a lot of sleeping slaves locked away." He opened his book and went back to reading, deliberately turning his back on Arran.

Arran wanted to get up, but forced himself to stay. "That is not how you persuade someone," he said deliberately. "Are you afraid to defend your views?"

This time when Gilead looked up there was a light of battle shining out of the pale eyes, and just a hint of warmth in his smile. "Let's talk," Gilead said.

Arran found the doctor outside the walls of the keep later that day. He had wandered up to the northern meadow and stood looking toward Landing, his eyes lost and sad.

Arran had a task, but it didn't mean he couldn't seek to perform a kindness as well. "I have received an inquiry from my cousin the king. He wishes to know of the sleeper's progress so that he may attend the king. You could come as well."

Dr. McCrary continued looking off into the distance. "Was I commanded—excuse me, invited?"

"No." It was Arran's belief that the king did not wish to force the old man's attendance by even a gentle suggestion if he did not wish to come. Arran had shared his thinking once with the doctor, who had laughed at him, but not explained.

"The sleeper needs a little more time," Dr. McCrary said. "He is not yet ready to travel." Now he did look at Arran, and said blandly, "It's his eyes."

Arran snorted. There was nothing wrong with Gilead's eyes. Arran had known full well that the sleeper had used the feigned sensitivity of his eyes as a pretext to reconnoiter the keep. "I will write the king that he is ready." Arran was equally bland. "We shall get him a hat."

They stood in silence for a moment, watching a pair of eagles circle each other. Their mewling reached them over the air. It was a strange and undignified sound for so majestic a pair. Dr. McCrary had once disputed their name, explaining that eagles did not look like that and did not have long goose-like necks, but his complaining had brought about no changes. No one cared what the old sleeper thought about birds. He had not been born on Nwwwlf.

"Robert," Arran finally said, "how is it that Gilead is educated? He is a soldier."

The older man quirked a grey eyebrow at Arran. "You are the snob, aren't you?"

Arran's pale skin flushed. "He understands both the sciences and political theory." Arran hadn't thought that he would be interested in the soldier. He would have much preferred another doctor, or, better yet, an engineer who could build the generators or create another reactor that powered the sleepers' quarters and then supply power to the valley. It fit with his dreams of understanding enough to build such things himself, and he had his eye on a certain waterfall.

He had expected Gilead to be like the men around the king, men who devoted their days to the sword and their nights to the king's halls. The king's six electric light bulbs were meager in comparison to the tantalizing glimpses offered by what was buried in the mountain.

The old man's head tilted, and both grey eyebrows rose. "You must have had quite the talk."

"He is not inarticulate. His mind holds an entire construct of individual liberties even though he served in the military."

The old man from Earth pursed his lips demurely. "Those were things our military used to protect."

"Not a king, I gather." Arran was surprised at how dry the words came out. He loved his king. Everyone did. Arran even held Clarence in personal affection, and knew that Clarence needed the work Arran did with the doctor. Clarence, Arran's second cousin, was a little more than ten years older than Arran, and was one of the few who had been kind to Arran as a child when he discovered books and the glories of the past. Most of Arran's family had no interest in such things.

It was an odd thought, living one's own life.

"I was raised the same as Gilead," McCrary observed. "With similar values—although I'm not used to thinking of violence as a possible solution to my problems. We're different there."

"But your education is far greater," Arran said. After the soliloquy on liberty, Gilead had started quizzing Arran about the resuscitation manual he was reading. It was clear that Gilead knew far less than McCrary or even Arran himself about the details of the process. Nonetheless, his questions were sound.

"He probably knows the basics of biology and chemistry from his school years, which were likely pretty similar to mine. I'll bet he knows a lot more ballistics than I do."

Arran digested this.

"Robert," Arran said, changing tacks, "is Gilead a Pan? Without the horns?"

"No," McCrary said firmly. "He is not. He is a soldier, born just the same as you or I."

"But?" Arran prompted.

McCrary's voice was now professorial. "But he has certain advantages that you and I do not."

"He learns very quickly," Arran said. One often received more answers if one did not ask a question.

"Like a two-year old," the doctor said. "They gave him a cocktail that restored the absorbent qualities of the mind of the human young. You ever see a two year old? You know how they learn language and what everything is around them so fast? It's a stage in individual human development, and then we lose it. Gilead got it back."

"The Pan do not have that?"

"I don't know. They were not my area, and I did not read much about them."

Arran wondered why Dr. McCrary lied. He didn't seem to know that Arran could see through him, that he had learned the other's tells. His voice would trail off in rampant uncertainty, and often he would bite his lower lip. The doctor did both now.

"Could you create that cocktail?"

"If you get rid of feudalism, figure out capitalism, and let me direct the chemistry research, sure. You'd have lots of other good stuff, too. Not to mention indoor plumbing." The old man sighed.

Arran ignored all this. He had heard it before, and would dearly have loved to better understand the magic of capitalism, but it made no sense to him. Man worked for the good of the king, not for himself. Witness the current situation.

"Will you be going with him?" McCrary asked.

"I think I should," Arran said. "Somebody needs to look after him."

Dr. McCrary smiled. "I don't think so. I think that young man can look after himself just fine."

The door was deep in the belly of the mountain on which the keep perched. Behind the door lay the sleeping quarters of those who had planned, like Gilead and Andrea had, to settle on a rough but civilized new world, terraformed to Earth normal. Instead, the people behind the door lay entombed on a strange world that they had not intended to reach, and looked to have no chance of being let out individually, much less with their families.

Gilead assumed the settlers had awakened the children and, maybe, their parents with them. He hoped there were no parentless children behind the door.

There was a keypad lock from Gilead's era, where one pushed the buttons in a particular order. It did not worry him. He closed his eyes briefly and thought about the slowly scrolling list that the doctor had let him see. He had searched it in his mind many times for Andrea's name, but now he looked for something else. He knew he had seen it, and, sure enough, the old man or someone before him had included the numbers to the door in the list.

Gilead came well equipped for his expedition. He had a scope from the lab, taken at an hour when he did not expect either Arran or McCrary to return. He had last seen Arran tracking the doctor out to the meadow, and they would likely head to dinner in the front hall next.

Gilead had also, miracle of miracles, found a portable, electrically charged flashlight in McCrary's lab. Gilead's didn't have his own light or his blaster although his kit still held any number of other useful items, including a line and a Tool ™. The comm did him no good in any practical way, although he had charged it and tested it, faintly but foolishly hoping. There'd been no one out there.

He didn't like carrying the Nwwwlf lanterns, which were clearly a fire hazard and gave anyone who had spent time in a spacecraft the willies. He particularly did not want to carry one that evening, when the light tickle of smoke could alert anyone to his presence. He sometimes suspected that the Marss couldn't smell it, so used to it were they, but he meant to take no risks. Not when he was heading for the sleeper's quarters and Andrea.

He took a breath and tried McCrary's numbers on the keypad. The door unlatched.

He pushed it open. It creaked alarmingly, and he swore under his breath. This, he had not anticipated, but should have, given the condition of the metal in the damp air. Here, in the depths of the mountain, the air was cold and moist. He worried about the effect that would have on the sleepers' cells. Damp wasn't good for machinery.

He stood in a reconstructed starship corridor. It made him think he'd found the right door.

His shoulders itched like they did sometimes before battle, but the rest of him felt light and buoyant as if they'd turned the gravity off for no reason. She had to be in here.

He marveled at the seamless insertion of technology into living rock. The original settlers had taken their screwed up idea very seriously, bringing down parts of the starship to support the lunacy. What kind of people had thought this a good idea when they would have needed all hands for battling the wilderness? Maybe it had started simply as a precaution. They didn't want everyone to wake up and die of some alien bug all at once. Nwwwlf was neither a terraformed planet nor a tested one. The settlers were the testers, and seeing what the bugs were like might have been sensible before waking all the people.

But leaving them there. That was different.

Not unlike a morgue, the sleeping cells were stacked, but these had room for the occupants to sit up. The lower ones were ankle high, the ones above a little over waist height. Each had a large number on it, and he swore. How the hell was he supposed to find Andrea this way? He brought his light closer, and saw that someone had scrawled in handwriting names on many of them beneath the numbers. The person had scratched them in with a knife, it looked like, and as he inspected each one, he saw names from top to bottom.

He stood up from a crouch, and wondered if it had been McCrary who had put the names in. It might have been his small and only act of defiance.

He frowned. There were almost two hundred cells in the corridor, and he had only recognized one name. They were not arranged alphabetically, and the numbers followed no recognizable logic. Worse, as he walked down the corridor, the names stopped. Now he saw only numbers, and he had not looked at the numbers on the doctor's screen with their corresponding names.

This time he recognized the frustration coursing through him. It matched the mania he had felt before he went haring off in unknown territory and started scaling the side of an unfamiliar mountain on an uncharted planet.

He surveyed the long corridor stretching ahead of him, longer than a football field. How many sleepers had they left in here? He wandered to the door at the end and tried the handle. It opened easily onto a cold room full of medical supplies. He granted that the locals were unsparing in their use of electric power for their strange fetish.

He trudged back up the long corridor to the exit, and, leaving the room, eyed the door. Leaving it open would tell the next person who happened along that someone had entered. Closing it would be loud. Someone might not happen along, and one couldn't stand around all day. He reached out, closed it, and it screamed like a dying cat.

He moved swiftly back down the stone corridor,

treading lightly, but moving fast. He heard booted feet and voices. Someone had come to rescue the cat.

The corridor had its share of turns, but no hiding places—no recessed alcoves, no welcoming doors. If he walked out brazenly, they would know he had opened one of the doors and perhaps set a guard. He could not afford that. He did not know how to awaken the civilian sleepers, and had no wish to be denied McCrary's company.

Since the only way out led past the voices, he retreated farther into the belly of the mountain. He set his light very low, and shielded it with his body. He had no wish to fall down some natural declivity or worse. For one thing, it would make a lot of noise. Maybe, if he died, they would awaken Andrea. Probably not. She was enhanced, too, but the assumptions about women mirrored those of Earth's ancient past, not one where technology bridged the physical gap between the sexes.

There were no more doors, either of composites or wood, and he became convinced, whether by smell or the feel of the wall, that he had entered a path more ancient than the presence of man on Nwwwlf. The voices were very distant, and he stopped. He played the light briefly on his surroundings, and saw a branching of the way. No, he had no desire to proceed. More interestingly, there was a hole in the opposite wall. He could hide there if he had to, and let them wonder which branch he had taken.

He turned off his light and waited in a blackness that pressed on his eyeballs and filled his nose and ears. He didn't like it.

After what seemed an eternity, he became convinced that the sounds of people had gone. There had been no breaks in the wall, and he was able to return in the direction in which he had come.

No one waited at the door to the sleeping quarters,

and he breathed a sigh of relief. He maintained his caution. They might wait for him up ahead. He paused every few steps, listening. He no longer dared use his light, and tucked it safely into his belt.

When he saw the light ahead, he breathed another sigh of relief. The more populated hall lay ahead. He merely had to reach it and act all nonchalant. Everything would be fine.

It was when he surreptitiously peered around the corner into the lighted hall that he came nose to nose with Etienne's grinning face. "Got you," that gentlemen said. "You may come quietly, or I can drag you by the heels."

Gilead's protestations of being lost fell on deaf ears. Arran had received a message from the king, inquiring as to the sleeper's health, and, if Gilead could prowl the corridors beneath the mountain, Arran could send a message back that the king's new prize was on his way. Arran ignored his own worry that Gilead might have found his way into the sleepers' quarters. Gilead could not have gotten through the locked door. Indeed, he hoped that now that Gilead had seen the futility of reaching what he sought, he might abandon that search.

Cruelly, Arran pointed out that Gilead didn't have much in the way of luggage, so packing should not be too large a chore. Arran cheerfully confined him to his quarters until they could all depart for First Landing the next day.

Gilead didn't castigate himself. Although he had never gone back to check Andrea's exact location on the list, he now knew where the sleepers were kept. Every little bit of information helped, and he had learned this just in time, before the king's summons arrived.

He contemplated pretending to be sick, but Arran, at least, would not believe him. There was a youngster with too much power. He reminded Gilead of certain new lieutenants he had served under. Gilead himself, however, needed to slow down and gain these people's trust, make them believe that he was on board with their wacky wackiness. He wasn't even sure, if he thought about it, that he could trust McCrary. The doctor had let Gilead see the list of sleepers, and Gilead was sure that had been deliberate, but McCrary had reason to be cautious, with his family at stake, and maybe now regretted what was probably an impulsive gesture. No, Gilead told himself, he could take nothing and no one for granted. He would have to be sent back to Fort Stampo, preferably on an errand for the king. Maybe Gilead could get the king to insist that another sleeper be awakened. Regardless of whatever scheme might or might not work, one thing was for sure, Gilead would need a lot more information on everything from the extent of the human-friendly biome to the political scene. He might get only one shot at waking his wife and the others, and he meant to get it right.

His companions the next day included Arran, in his obvious capacity as Gilead's baby sitter, several guardsmen, two women who were wives to the guards and beside themselves with excitement, and Etienne, who had been exiled from First Landing for some reason a few years earlier and was now thrilled to return. Arran told Gilead at the start of the ride, when Etienne was safely far away, that the large guard hoped to ingratiate himself with the king or his court and return from his rustication.

The journey itself, on horseback, was not difficult, and far more pleasant than his attempts to assay the mountain. Nwwwlf, although Earth-like, was not Earth. What should have been blue was green, and what should have been green was blue. Always, there were undertones of lime, in the sky, in the grasses, and buried deep in the blue of the trees. Once they were out of the mountains they passed farmers' fields edged in scrappy stunted things that looked like live oak. Winged mammals rose out of them in great flocks as they approached, befuddling Gilead's sense of what was right for any living creature.

He had spent three years subjective of his service on Darling, part of a pair of terraformed worlds in a single solar system. The inhabitant's of Darling's southern continent warred with their neighbors to the north. This mattered to Earth—which had sent Gilead and Andrea's unit to settle the matter—because the northern neighbors wanted large reimbursements and resettlement, and the colony corporations never wanted to be seen to give in to such demands. It was cheaper to send mercenaries to defend them, than to relocate a population from a continent.

Darling had looked like Earth. Gilead's other missions had also been to terraformed worlds. Nwwwlf was his first truly alien sojourn.

He turned over and over in his mind how he could get back to the fort. He needed the doctor to train him in the safer and slower resuscitation techniques. He could use a combat wake on any of the other soldiers, but the civilian sleepers weren't primed for such a fast wake. Arran most likely wouldn't help. Gilead also needed McCrary to let him access all the data banks so he could find Andrea.

He dreamt of her at night. Sometimes the dreams were better than waking, full of laughing and the warmth of her skin. Otherwise, his fears haunted him, and he woke from the sight of her wasted form, dead in a cell that could double as a coffin.

She would have found this new world a treat. All

he got from it was that she wasn't in it. At least, not awake. If he woke her, they could head out into the wilderness, form their own farm, and raise their family away from this madness. They'd have to steal some chickens, and maybe a cow or two, but he hadn't yet learned what besides chicken provided an effective converter of Nwwwlf flora for people.

Andrea would find that interesting. She was the daughter of farmers, and he had found her intriguing when he first met her in boot camp. When joining the service pretty much guaranteed eventual permanent separation from one's family and friends, from all and everything one knew, whether for reasons fatal or relativistic, almost everyone who joined was fleeing something. His friend Llew had left behind grinding poverty, and Mason the same. Going by his first week, only Gilead came from a happy family who both loved him and could afford him. Only Gilead had no reason other than a desire to see the stars to be there. And, he had wanted to defend Earth from Mars, but that bit of posturing had ended right after Gilead had joined up.

Andrea Fielding had not had the haunted, hunted eyes of the others. Nor did she come from a politically connected family so that she only had to endure a stint in boot before going on to greater things. She was another child of the middle class, and from a family with land.

"But the thing is," she'd told him once, "even with the farm, my family was always about to lose it. Someone could always say the government had a better idea of how to use it, better than what we were doing with it. It wasn't really ours."

"You had title," Gilead had protested. He, too, was a child of the middle class and knew such things.

Andrea had scoffed. "No one was going to take your

parent's house in the suburbs. We were in danger because we had a lot."

"So your parents sent you here?" Gilead had been disbelieving, even at eighteen.

"No," Andrea's dark winged eyebrows had drawn down over her blue eyes. "But my mother spent a lot of time reading about the terraformed worlds, comparing their constitutions, figuring which would be the best to go to if only we had the money. My father hated it that she did that because having the money would mean the county had taken our land and 'paid' us for it. It had happened to several neighbors. She always said she just wanted to be ready when they did."

Andrea shook her head. They stood outside the obstacle course, waiting their turn. Gilead had taken to standing near her when he had the chance. He liked the way she firmed her lower lip back up whenever she tilted her head to look up at him, as if otherwise it would part naturally. This only happened when she spoke to him, he had been pleased to see.

The Mississippi sky was a bright blue, but the sun a wintry cold. The air moved what little there was of her black hair.

"I think we're here for the same reason," he had said.

"To become colonists?" she had asked.

When he'd nodded, she'd smiled.

He had known then, and he had been right.

Back in the present, Gilead resolved, that when he got all the sleepers out, they could start their own settlement, with no king, just plain, old, unromantic democracy. He would not run for office.

Arran interrupted Gilead's introspection. "Would you care for some guidance?"

"In what?" Gilead asked warily.

"In etiquette."

"Do I need that?"

Arran turned in his saddle as his mount plodded on. "Most certainly."

Gilead spent the next hour taking instructions on how and when to bow, the imperative need to bow to the king, what to address various august personages as, and how not to make an ass of himself otherwise. Gilead's sisters would have loved it, but Gilead found it difficult to take seriously, and he could find no way of mentioning this challenge without drawing more attention to his need for etiquette guidance.

He listened with only half his mind. The rest was keenly conscious that with every step he left Andrea farther and farther behind. After all they had been through together, after all they had survived, these people meant for him never to see her again. He had his own plans, of course.

He watched the landscape. He noted every turn in the dirt road, every hillock, and every long meadow filled with low flowers and swarms of insects. The terrain was very flat now. In the distance, he saw the sheen of water. It reflected the sky in a white but fuzzy haze, as if it were full of rushes and grass. Lumps large enough to see from a great distance moved slowly in the water and Arran told him that he was looking at a toadfat farm. Toadfats were the source of lamp oil. Arran understood them to be much larger than the toads of earth, and to provide something like whale blubber at maturity. They liked water.

"And, look," Arran said, as they rounded a low hill, "you will now get to practice your new skills."

A party of riders trotted toward them, more colorful than Gilead's own. The men wore the indigo of Arran's tunic, which now took on the indicia of a uniform, or, at least a sign that he belonged to a group of some sort.

The wind picked up and lifted thin, gauzy veils from the heads of two of the women in the group ahead. As they drew near, Gilead was able to make out seven or eight people astride, their voices carrying in the clear air with the tenor of joking and teasing.

"Convoy, ho," called out the leader, and drew his own party to a halt. He was young, not much older than Gilead, with a head of yellow hair that fell straight and shining and fine just below his ears. His hair looked as if it had been cut around a bowl placed on his head, which Gilead decided to take as yet another sign of the descent back into savagery that these people had indulged. The man's eyes were strikingly blue, and high cheekbones gave them a slight tilt. It was hard to tell when he was seated on a horse, but he looked not just strong but powerful. If he wasn't the king, he could have played one on a video.

"My lord," Arran called happily.

Gilead's group approached, and pulled to a stop a few meters away. Except for Gilead, they all dismounted and dropped to one knee.

This was when Gilead realized he was well and truly trapped in a futuristic, dystopian setting. This was the guy, Clarence Rex, lord of the landing, the big guy in the valley, he who sought to fight the Pan (what a man), and the one who kept sleepers sleeping. Gilead found himself filled with fury. If this was, indeed, the person who was so powerful that they called him a king, he was the one responsible right now for Andrea's imprisonment.

Gilead's entire body trembled, and it took all his self-control not to launch himself from his horse at the guy.

Gilead felt Arran's eyes on him, but did not take his own from the king's.

"You are Gilead Tan?" the king inquired. If he saw the fury in Gilead's eyes, his own showed only mild amusement.

"I am," Gilead said. "And, I'm pleased to meet you." He did not look at them, but the persons in the king's escort were doing a lot of moving nervously, going by the amount of unnecessary stepping coming from their horses. Two people were whispering.

"Why is that?" Clarence asked. "It is not as if you show me any courtesy."

As a rule, Gilead tried not to talk when he was seeing red, but he was in a country with bad rules, and so he ignored his own. "You are holding my wife hostage. I've only once met any kidnappers"—there was that ugly group on Needham—"and I offered them no courtesies either."

The king's eyes were bright with laughter. It only made Gilead more furious. "And what did you offer them instead? Or, should I not ask?"

"We shot most of them," Gilead said bluntly. "We arrested and jailed the three who lived."

The king turned to his courtiers. "I should not have asked." They laughed, but without much conviction. A wind came back, almost like a live thing, and moved the long scarves across the women's faces.

Arran was holding the reins of Gilead's horse right behind the bit. His face was white, and he looked as furious as Gilead felt. "Get off your horse," he hissed.

"Let," said Gilead slowly, "go."

Clarence raised a hand. "We have a newcomer. Let us be tolerant of his differences." His eyes narrowed, and his face lost its good humor. "I am not tolerant of the insults."

He turned his attention to Arran, gestured, and wheeled his horse. Arran and his company remounted, the guards closing around Gilead in visible hostility. Arran rode ahead to the king's side, where they started talking in low voices to one another, their backs to

Gilead. The courtiers rode in a loose line between Gilead's minders and Arran and the king.

He could hear them. He had let everyone see his strength and speed. He had no doubt that they knew of it, and that his physical prowess was part of the reason they had picked a soldier. He did not consider it wise to share all his abilities.

The king's voice was quiet and steady, with no sign of anger. He asked a lot of questions about Gilead, and Arran gave him thorough answers. Apparently, Arran had found many aspects of Gilead's recovery startling in the extreme and planned to present a scientific paper on Gilead's physiology. Gilead had visions of himself pinned to a piece of cardboard for display.

Arran also told him of Gilead's mysterious disappearance down a certain corridor, and Etienne's conviction that he had found the sleeping quarters. This last bit of information drew a look back at Gilead from his majesty.

The courtiers rode quietly, their earlier gaiety vanished. They strained to hear the king and Arran, but lacked Gilead's gifts.

It was only when the king started asking about Gilead's wife that the fury returned. His horse picked up its pace, but his guards closed around him, and he was the only one unarmed. He resumed a less hurried trot.

The city rose ahead of them. The starship had brought construction materializers in its hold. Although farms and houses sprawled amidst planted fields on this side of the river, the buildings on the other side were a strange combination of local stone and seamless 'crete and plast that looked very much like home. The walls must have been built later, when the materializers no longer worked, for they were hewn from blocks of stone taller than Gilead. It was impressive, and he could not imagine how they had accomplished such a feat without modern machinery, although, perhaps, he should revise his use of the word modern. What he needed to yearn for, instead, was his old-fashioned past.

Arran rode back to Gilead as they passed through an array of close-set wooden houses leading to a large bridge—clearly built by the first settlers showing some foresight. There were clangs of metal, and the smell of smoke increased. Down a road perpendicular to their path he saw what might have been a foundry.

Chickens and dogs scattered before the horse's hooves, and people stopped what they were doing to watch. Men removed their hats at the sight of the king.

Gilead wondered briefly what the king did with those who failed to follow the rules of etiquette. Everyone was pretty compliant on the road to the bridge.

"It would be a great favor to me," Arran said stiffly, "if you would behave. And, you must not accuse him of kidnapping again. He is safeguarding the legacy of our ancestors, as did those who came before him, including his father."

Gilead studied his minder. Arran liked the king. Gilead did not. Regardless, he knew he had to control his temper. Getting himself locked up would not help him to free Andrea and the others.

"You will see him again this evening. You must follow my etiquette instructions."

"Sure, Arran," Gilead said absently. "Sure I will."

They bathed him. He was glad of that, but marveled at the physical labor involved in obtaining heated water. The servants who brought it were pleased to be near the part of the building with pipes. The pipes to his room in the palace only carried cold water, which he didn't understand but was the way of things.

The palace itself was one of the original buildings built by the settlers from the starship. From the looks of it, it had been a laboratory or a school, with many rooms off hallways in a giant rectangle. Later generations added to it, colored it, and changed the additions, but the fundamental core remained solid and unchanged. That seemed like sufficient legacy to Gilead.

After the bath, which he assured the sternly handsome woman who wanted to help that he could perform without her, he found new clothes laid out for him. He had gotten used to the white pirate shirt they had given him, but he preferred his own clothes. His original weight allotment for the interstellar voyage had run to underwear, two pair of fitted dress pants, two flannel shirts, one good shirt, a pair of loafers, and another pair of athletic shoes. He liked civilian clothes, but had meant to purchase a real wardrobe upon arrival at New Mars. He had them all with him, and thought of them as he surveyed the offerings laid out on his bed.

There was a white pirate shirt, of course, and a pair of what he supposed he would call breeches. A long, sleeveless tunic in indigo—the king's color he had been told—and a long jacket, also in indigo, looked freshly pressed. A pair of ankle boots completed the look.

A freestanding mirror confirmed that the breeches were mildly obscene, and he pulled on the tunic gratefully. A knock sounded on the door, and a terrified looking young man stood there. "Please, sir, allow me to help. I am Teth, your valet."

Over his arm hung a towel and another pair of breeches.

Gilead pointed at the breeches. "Are those any bigger than the ones I've got on?"

Arran showed up in back of the boy. "No. And you're fine. Keep getting dressed." He strolled to a chair by the fire, and seated himself, his fingers steepled in front of his chin. "You need to think on some things, Gilead. You are not irreplaceable. If you push things too far, you'll land in jail or worse." Arran's resemblance to a certain young lieutenant had grown more pronounced the closer they had gotten to First Landing. Now, it was approaching borderline unbearable.

"Ostracism?" Gilead asked hopefully.

Arran surveyed Gilead through hooded eyes. It was as if proximity to the king had filled him with new power, and his interest in Gilead had changed from one of delighted interest to concern that Gilead would embarrass him. That mattered to young lieutenants. "No, because then we couldn't wake another one of you. Something more permanent."

"Can't the king just change that requirement?" Gilead asked. He kept his eyes closed while the valet toweled his hair.

"No. It is the law." Arran's voice sounded displeased, as if Gilead was trying to be stupid.

"The king isn't above the law?"

"No."

"Who makes the law?"

Arran's sigh reached him clearly. "No one makes the law. It just is."

"Let me try again. Who decides the law? When people disagree."

"At the highest level, the king, of course."

Gilead suffered his hair to be brushed. "Now you're messing with me," he said.

"This law is very clear," Arran said. "No disputes come up around it."

"What if I fled and escaped to the Pan?" Gilead asked, just to be difficult. "Could you wake another sleeper?"

Arran was actively scowling. "I don't know. That hasn't happened before."

Gilead let the valet lift his chin. When the youth reached for a piece of cloth, Gilead dropped his chin, and the boy put it back up. He wrapped the cloth, which was silky and soft and the first nice clothing Gilead had encountered, around Gilead's neck. "So it's not that clear, the fifty-year limit."

He looked in the mirror and saw that Arran also had a silky cloth around his neck. They were both quite stylish, he had no doubt. Andrea would have laughed if she could have seen him. Arran's scowl lightened. "Enough sophistry. We must go."

He rose and led Gilead through a series of corridors covered in carpet, down stairs made of wood, past painted pictures and arched windows, and on into what Arran called the new wing of the king's palace.

They arrived at a new throne room. Large chandeliers covered in crystal and floating balls of toadfat oil blazed from the ceiling far above the throng of people. At the other end of the room was a raised dais, with two large chairs upon it. The crowded room was warm with the press of flesh. The women wore full skirts and heart shaped tops that crushed their breasts into compliance. Their shoulders were bare and gleamed in the light from multiple lanterns. The men were dressed much as Gilead was, but in colors that would have competed well with an array of football teams.

Live musicians played a whole lot of stringed instruments off to the side of the room. He wondered if there was dancing, or if there was a law about that.

As someone who was used to the temporal vagaries of space travel, he had long ago accepted that he carried his family and culture with him, and, if he was lucky, with the few who started with and stayed with him. Like Andrea and his friends. What he had not expected was this lunatic regression to Earth's past. Maybe McCrary was right that democracy and civilization were an aberration in humanity's history. Add one strongman and a group of frightened people to the mix and you could derail everything.

He was receiving smiles and nods as Arran worked their way to a line approaching the pair of thrones. He could hear his name running in murmurs through the room. Women with lively eyes touched his shoulder, and one said, "Welcome, Gilead Tan. Thank you for your sacrifice."

His eyebrows went up, but he only smiled and nodded in return. He could feel Arran at his side, quivering like a greyhound, worried, no doubt, that Gilead would repeat his gross violations of etiquette. Gilead hadn't made up his mind about that. He could not kneel. He just couldn't. A free man knelt to no one, and he couldn't undermine his position on that front, even if only in his own mind. However, here might not be the best place to repeat his accusations of kidnapping, and he was already regretting his earlier comments. As a tactician, he should know well enough not to give away his position so quickly. As a man, his anger took hold of his tongue. He would not kneel, but he would not speak out. Not yet.

The men to either side of him introduced themselves. He filed the names away in case of later need. There was the Lord of This, and the Lord of That, Sir Whosis and the Honorable Him, the bureaucrat who administered the toadfat farms for the king and was shaped like a toad himself. The bureaucrat had some sort of complex about the six electric light bulbs in the room and tried to talk about the importance of safeguarding them. "The king is the steward of electrical power," the man explained. "Until everyone can have the bulbs, which are very hard to make, only the king has them. In fact, when you think about it, the electricity is a wasteful luxury. The light is just as good from a toadfat lamp, and does not require these complex intermediate steps to achieve light."

Gilead decided he couldn't cross this cultural divide, and made no attempt to do so.

A pair of lurking women just dimpled, their eyes promising later introductions. It was mildly creepy.

Cellular pressure finally ejected Arran and Gilead to the front of the throng, and he faced the pair of thrones. A master of ceremonies clothed in all the colors of the rainbow announced him. "Gilead Tan, Sleeper from Earth and the Landing, formerly of the 34th Marines of the WesHem Confederacy of Earth." Who had known that he held such titles?

The room was very quiet. He stared at the king. This was where he was supposed to drop to one knee. The king stared back, an amused light in his eyes. There was something else there, too, not so amused and harder.

Gilead took a step forward, hand outstretched. Shaking hands was courteous. He could do that.

He had been focused only on the king, but something about the woman at his side made him look at her, something about the line of her jaw, the shell of her ear. Her forehead was clear, her dark hair a complicated mass of braids on top of her head, but the sketch of her brows winging away from her eyes, the deep blue of the eyes themselves, and the straight nose with the slight tilt, the long, full mouth, these were all features he knew as well as he knew the rest of her. This was Andrea, the women he knew and loved. No wonder he hadn't found her in the sleepers' hall. She was seated on a throne.

His hand fell to his side. He forgot the king.

They had gone under together for their journey. He had awakened expecting to find her at his side or to be at hers very shortly. In his own mind, it had been a few short weeks since last he had seen her, and here she was, seated at the side of the king.

He was having trouble breathing, and his whole body was filled with a heat that tortured him like true fire. She had betrayed him.

His tunnel vision obscured the rest of the room, and he could only see her face, the black hair, the ruby lips, the skin white as snow. And he saw the puzzled eyes, and that she didn't know him.

"Andrea?" he heard himself ask. "Is it you?"

"I am Mary. I am the queen," the woman said, and although the timbre of her voice made clear that she was Andrea's clone somehow, the accent was that of the people of this valley.

His mind went utterly blank, for how long, he didn't know, so he didn't hear the murmuring of the people at his back, see the frown growing on the face of the king, or feel Arran's hand on his elbow gripped tightly. After long moments, when his brain rebooted and spit out the answer, it was more unbearable than that she sat here before him.

His wife was long gone. She must have been awakened in the landing, and this woman was one of her descendants. Andrea had not awakened Gilead. She had acquiesced in the madness, and borne children to another man. And here sat her granddaughter many times removed.

The horror of it drove him not to one knee, but to two, and he sank back on his heels, only his hands on his thighs holding him upright.

CHAPTER 5

I T WAS A WEEK AFTER the debacle before their majesties. Arran had dispatched a swift rider to the mountain fastness, and Robert McCrary, more slowly, had been brought to the palace.

He and the doctor stood on the little balcony outside Gilead's room, watching the scene in the courtyard below. Gilead, it appeared, dealt with grief through physical activity, and could spend hours training in the courtyard. He made regular inquiries after real weapons, as if the answer would change the fifth time he asked, and someone would produce the energy weapons he insisted they must have. Arran knew of no such cache. Dr. McCrary had been able to put a stop to that, at least, assuring Gilead that the planet lacked the infrastructure for their manufacture, maintenance, or charging.

"He's not sick," Dr. McCrary said.

"He is heartsick," Arran said. "I called for you so that we could claim he had a fever."

"So I'm here for nothing." The physician put his hands on his lower back and tried to stretch. He was too old for the maneuver. "Just a show."

"I am sorry. The king did not want the people to believe this sleeper a weak man." Arran himself had been shocked at Gilead's reaction, although grateful the man had performed a proper obeisance. To the onlookers, it appeared that the sleeper had bent the knee. "I believe that he meant to free his wife once he figured out how, but the queen looks just like his wife, which means she was awakened at the landing."

"And she left him there," Dr. McCrary said. "She didn't get him out."

Arran was surprised. "How could she have?" Women did not excel at such endeavors.

"She was a soldier, too," the older man reminded him. "Things were different in my day, when we had the technology for people to make more choices."

"She could have done that?" Arran gestured to the courtyard below. Gilead Tan, stripped to the waist and streaked with dust and sweat, his dark hair plastered to his head, grappled with his most recent opponent, a man the size of a small mountain. The mountain's nose had been broken many times—he must have been slow in defending his face on a regular basis—and he was no beauty, but his sinews popped and flashed as if his muscles were made of living snakes, and when he planted his feet he would survive a building falling on him. Gilead's tactics were to let the other man tire himself, and the sleeper didn't let him close. He was the opposite of the mountain, a swiftly moving mammal, lithe and deadly, and beautiful with it. All the women watched him, and the looks were more than just because he was the latest revived sleeper.

"No," McCrary said slowly, as if considering what he wanted to share, and forgetting how much he already had shared with Arran in his lonely life in the mountain. "The enhancements helped the women, but the real equalizers were the weaponry. Which you don't have anymore."

"The king is happy with all of this," Arran said. "The sleeper is serving his purpose. He is as strong and swift as the Pan, and will be a good champion for the king."

McCrary scratched his nose. "I don't know how

much Gilead knows about medieval warfighting. Not sure how much use he's going to be aside from single combat."

"He will protect the king," Arran said simply. That was enough for him. Someone needed to protect this king. The king was the only one pushing to rid the country of the Pan and their depredations. Arran very much wanted him to succeed, despite the opposition of certain nobles, including Arran's own father. His father should have shared Arran's reasons, but chose to forget what he could do nothing about, and so forgot his own lost child. "That is enough."

Arran admitted that it was too bad that Gilead's desire to awaken them all couldn't be allowed. Those sleeping people had so much knowledge in their heads. Waking them one by one preserved the memory of Earth, but waking them all might allow them to rebuild their past.

"And there's his propaganda value," McCrary said drily.

"His inspirational value," Arran said, equally dry, and very sure of himself. They understood each other, and neither cared about the other's opinion.

Gilead had not meant these people to see his grief. In his heart, Andrea was only a week lost to him because Gilead had not accepted even the possibility that the Marss would succeed in keeping them separated. The double shock had been almost a physical blow, and he had suffered a fever for a day, which Arran, with the heartlessness of a twenty-year old male, coldly informed him was a bug. Neither mentioned that he was heartsick. Gilead figured Arran was embarrassed for him.

Andrea had figured so much into all his plans for

the future. They had endured so much together in the service, and appreciated so thoroughly all the easy sweetness of civilian life. No matter how difficult the frontiers were, they were no match for being shot at, wounded on a regular basis, and fearing the loss of your lover or friends at a moment's notice. Having finally achieved the sweetness, he had had it for all of a few months. Andrea had had it—for how long? A lifetime? Did she die young in childbirth, like other primitive women? How bad had it been in the early days with the ship's resources still to hand?

His other questions were worse. How could she have left him sleeping? Had it been that impossible? Had they used force on her?

The only possibility that made him more miserable than the latter was the former—and vice versa.

He asked to see the library, but it was all on paper. None of the digital records, which were what had recorded the landing, could be read anymore. The paper records were not easily searchable.

He didn't train to suit the king. He trained for the distraction it brought him, and with the thought in the back of his head that he would kill them all. This kind of thinking was not actually helpful, because the people he really wanted to kill were long dead. The current generation was just brainwashed by its ancestors' idiocy.

He still meant to wake the others, but the decision was no longer an exhilarating goal, just a grim determination to do his duty by his comrades and friends.

He couldn't figure what had led to the decision to let the sleepers lie. The doctor had nothing to offer but speculation, but they agreed there must have been some Greatest Number cultists aboard the starship, seeking to bring their oppressive approach to the settlements.

They were able to justify anything so long as it might offer the greatest good for the greatest number, hence the name. The individual had no sanctity. His life belonged to others, and a person had an endless claim on the lives of others, but very few rights in his own.

Maybe, if there had been food shortages or disease attending the landing, there would have been voices raised demanding that more mouths to feed not be awakened.

"Also," McCrary pointed out as he checked Gilead's vital signs shortly after arriving from the mountain, "you'll notice that almost all you soldiers—the men, at least—were left sleeping. There had to have been some dissent, and if the soldiers had sided with the dissenters, the whole plan might have failed."

"We might have been handy tools of oppression," Gilead said bitterly. He lay on his back and addressed the ceiling. His fever was gone, but McCrary checked him every day, probably to keep up the pretense that he had been sick when he fell to his knees in front of the king.

McCrary raised his eyebrows. "But if the plan, whatever it was, was working without you, why take the chance?" He shone a small light into Gilead's eyes, leaving stars on the retina. He sat back. "You're fine. Your health remains excellent, and you've persuaded me and everyone within ten miles that you are the most powerful man alive."

"Except for the Pan." Gilead swung his legs off the bed and reached for a shirt. "About them. Why the hostility? They were going to New Mars, too, weren't they?"

"Yes. And the settlement companies always tried not to put incompatibles together. Not that people couldn't become incompatible, but why ask for trouble?"

He pulled himself off the stool and moved to the

chair by the fireplace. Gilead felt the doctor eying him with clinical interest. Gilead knew he looked different than the men he faced in the courtyard. His muscles were long, not bound, and he had an elasticity that allowed great speed. Gilead knew he was like the Pan.

The older man's answer was slow in coming. "I don't know what caused the rift, but they struck off on their own very early and were not heard from for a long time. They do steal children from the Marss; I suspect it's because they don't have enough of their own."

Gilead eyed the doctor in a considering sort of way. His pale eyes were bleak. "Maybe I'll go see what the Pan are like. I'm not too crazy about things around here."

McCrary was on his feet in an instant. "Don't talk like that," he hissed. "If someone heard you, even your status as a sleeper would not save you. They all hate the Pan or have reason to. It's like saying you're off to see a bunch of child kidnappers."

Gilead's eyebrows went up. The old man had to understand the irony of what he had just said.

As if reading his mind, McCrary said testily, "Yes, yes. I note and appreciate the hypocrisy. You would like to have been long dead."

"With my wife," Gilead corrected him. "Long dead would just be an ancillary benefit at this point."

McCrary looked embarrassed, as if he had forgotten he was speaking to someone whose grief was still fresh.

What made it worse for Gilead was that it was so unexpected. Had Andrea died in the service, it would have been hell, true enough. But they had avoided that. They had mustered out safely and had been about to start their real life, the one they had gone through so much to reach. He shut if off, for perhaps the fifth time that day. He couldn't think about her.

Gilead was having trouble thinking about much of anything. When he wasn't exhausting himself with physical labor, he thought about Andrea, so he spent as much time exhausting himself as he could. He was even starting to master the long bow. His skin wasn't, but that was what bandages were for.

"Also," McCrary said carefully, "you need to be aware of your position."

"My position?" Gilead's mind drew a blank. It did that a lot these days. "I don't have a position."

"You are the sleeper. You represent Earth and the lost past. That means something around here."

Kind of like he and Andrea had represented the Earth they knew to each other. "I did not volunteer for that job. I've done my service."

"Regardless, it's your position here. But, just as I'm a sleeper and a doctor, you are a sleeper and a soldier. The king has plans for you."

"I am not leading anyone's armies into battle." That seemed perfectly clear to Gilead. He didn't understand why it should remain a mystery to everyone else.

"You have a large database of tactics and strategy in your head. But if you don't work out on that front, I understand you are at least slated to be the king's champion, which is a job title around here. All your training is useful for that, but there's more to it. You may be wondering why the king hasn't called for you."

Gilead gave him a hard look. "I can't tell you how much I don't care."

McCrary sighed. "Gilead, I'm sorry, but I have to warn you. The other thing is the queen."

Gilead didn't have anything to say to that.

McCrary moved over to the balcony and didn't look at the other man, but he pressed on. "Most people didn't notice, but some did. There is talk about how you couldn't take your eyes off her. How you ignored the king. That you knelt to her, not to Clarence."

"I guess that's kind of awkward for everyone," Gilead said.

The courtyard for practicing was muddy. It had rained the night before, and, with the sun rising over the hills, a fine mist lifted off the ground. Gilead eyed the mud with distaste. Today was a day for archery or a run. He had decent shoes for running. He might as well use them before they wore out. He had run before, and received strange looks, but he had located a park.

Now would be a good day to visit it. He started off running fast and light before the sun could turn the morning too hot. The palace stood on elevated ground set back almost a kilometer from the river. The settlers had shown a lot of faith in it not flooding. He wound his way through a maze of houses that crowded the hill on the eastern side away from the river.

At the bottom he turned north, and, around the long curve of a broader road, stretched the park, on a raised and flat stretch of ground. Someone had planted with care, and what looked like tall, skinny pine trees formed rows at the entrance, like a foreshortened plantation. They were only about six deep, a nod to order before the meandering began. Paths wandered randomly, around ponds and small hillocks in rusty lime, between closely planted alleys of flowering shrubs and tall indigo grasses. The park was very designed, and full of private spaces. Copses of trees hid birds, including, no doubt, the ever present chickens. He breathed in the sweetly fragrant air and sprinted. He was tempted to slow, but didn't dare. Slowing led to thinking.

Gilead didn't pay much attention to the people he trained with. There was one huge and hugely ugly enlisted man who was guaranteed to just about kill him any time they came in contact. They had called a draw with each other several times, because Gilead tended to reply with commensurate force. The sword was a different matter. The fellows with the swords spoke a lot better and tended to smell as if they had at least thought about bathing. The Middle Ages were squalid.

He saw one of the swordsmen now as his path entered a glade deep in shadow, sheltered from the early morning sun by tall trees all around it, the smell of resin strong. The other man sat astride a brown horse, a sword at his side. "Ho, sleeper," the man called out. Gilead remembered his name—Joshua Calhoun. He had met him, but never sparred. He'd watched him once, and thought him good.

"Mr. Calhoun," Gilead said, and raised a hand, not planning to stop.

"A word?" the gentlemen asked.

Gilead slowed. "A word it is."

"I understand you find the queen beautiful," Joshua said.

Now here was a trap. "She is lovely," Gilead agreed. He studied the man on horseback. He looked to be in his twenties, a red-haired man with a fire in his belly.

"Do you know who I am?" the horseman asked.

Gilead could answer this one. "That I do. You are Joshua Calhoun. We have met in the practice yard."

"I," said Joshua Calhoun, "am the king's champion. And I am displeased."

For the first time in many days, Gilead smiled. His wife would have called it his evil smile. He smiled because he recognized the situation. He understood this. It was very simple.

"And would the king's champion be more pleased if I'd said the queen was not lovely?" He didn't know if anyone had understood his reaction to the queen. Most had taken his horror as obedience to the king, the offer of the bended knee. He had called her Andrea out loud, but Arran, the only one to have heard and perhaps understood, didn't seem a gossipy sort, never mind McCrary's obvious, drunken lies on the topic.

The king's champion also smiled his evil smile. "Absolutely not. I would be aggrieved beyond measure."

"Thought so," Gilead said. He supposed he could climb up the horse—from the front—if the champion tried to run him down. He had not had many chances to encounter an armed attacker on horseback—maybe none. He supposed it would happen to him all the time now.

He sighed. "And you thought we should meet somewhere private, where you'd have no witnesses?" The man must have watched him this morning.

"No," the rider said. "I have witnesses."

Three men stepped out from behind the trees. They were all armed, but one carried an extra sword. The others arranged themselves at point around the glade in the wet grass. It was surreal. He recognized the context: the need to best a perceived rival, to establish dominance, to overcome the outsider. It was obvious that he was the object of all this attention, and, although it raised his heartbeat and his vision grew wide and expansive, it did not trouble him. He would, of course, take a sword with him on his next run, but now he just needed to avoid getting cut.

The choice of setting told him a lot. There were witnesses, but they were probably friends, and it wasn't the training yard of the palace where the whole world would see if Gilead bested the king's champion. And, if Gilead was never seen again, few would know why.

Joshua dismounted, pulling the reins over his mount's head and dropping the ends to the ground. "Stay," he said, and made a hand signal. The horse blinked and watched its rider stride into the middle of the glade.

"My displeasure with you demands satisfaction," the Marss announced.

Who talked like that, Gilead wondered. He folded his arms. "Maybe you should have a little chat with yourself. Explain how you don't get everything your way all the time. Shoot, even the king doesn't get everything he wants."

This brought a fire to Joshua's eyes. "I do not talk to myself. It is unhealthy."

Gilead shook his head sadly. "It's called introspection. Know thyself."

"You talk a lot. Perhaps too much." Joshua gestured to the man holding two swords. He was taller than Gilead, and of a weedy build, but his reach was long and his bearing solid. He crossed the grass, and held out the scabbard for Gilead to draw the sword from it. He tested it with a few passes, and the balance was good enough. They had not offered him the finest workmanship, but it would have been wasted on him. The tall man did not flinch or move away until Gilead stopped his carving shadows.

The sun reached the treetops and started throwing shadows that moved across Joshua's face, turning him into a clown, a redheaded harlequin. "What if I won't fight you?" Gilead said.

"I will kill you," the harlequin spoke. "And the king will be spared a man who looks at his queen as you do."

"Fair enough," Gilead said. "You having that view on things." He raised his sword, saluted, and lunged.

Joshua riposted with ease, his weapon an extension of his body, the mapping of it on his brain completed long ago. Gilead pulled back, weaving of wall of steel around himself, for although he lacked a lifetime of training, he didn't need it. He'd had a few weeks.

Joshua found the wall no deterrence, and, beating back Gilead's weapon, drove him out of the middle of the glade, closer to the reaching arms of an elongated tube of shrub covered in vines that spread into the grasses. The maneuver struck Gilead as unfair, and he stamped and parried, stamped and parried, holding his ground once he saw the way of things. The other man had Gilead's strength, and it was no easy task to stop his gains and still pay attention to his surroundings.

He stepped in a patch of soft ground, and his right foot shot back without his meaning it to. He stopped it, but not without a spasm that moved him too far to the right and allowed his opponent's edged weapon past his guard to pierce his chest or slice his arm in a gruesome moment of checkmate.

Time slowed as the sword closed in.

The only way he could stop it was with his arm, an arm to which he was firmly attached and had plans for involving the rest of his life. Later he pondered the state of medical care and whether losing the arm wouldn't have lost him his life as well, but in that instant he was resolved to surrender neither.

Still in his fugue state, he swiveled the hilt of the sword in his right hand, almost slicing his arm off himself, and, the wide blade flat against his arm, swiveled himself off-line on the precariously balanced foot, letting the blade of his own sword serve as an arm-guard with which he attacked the edge of Joshua's sword.

The clash sounded like kitchenware, discordant in the lime green glade, and birds screamed upwards, crying. Something slower mewled.

The red haired man was not going to let something so simple as a block, however unorthodox its execution, beat him back. He recovered instantly, but Gilead's sword-covered arm still had contact with the other's blade, as he rushed up it and drove the pommel of his own sword past the guard and into Joshua's wrist.

Joshua dropped his sword, and one of the men hollered as if in warning of what was already obvious. Gilead drove a kick into his belly and, grabbing the hilt with his other hand, jammed the pommel into Joshua's jaw. Joshua went down flat. Gilead took the sword back in his right hand, in the right direction, and placed the point of it at the other man's neck. Joshua blinked in the way that suggested he was seeing more stars than shone in the morning sky above.

"Are we done?" Gilead asked.

He had not lost track of the other men in the glade. They were not his friends, and he had no expectation of a fair fight, despite the loan of a weapon. He had not, however, thought to pay attention to the non-human creature that, giant haunches gathered beneath him, charged Gilead on the side away from its master.

Gilead redirected the long sword, but he didn't see what good it would do him. The animal, which looked to be closing on a tonne as well as on him, braked and settled back, raising its mighty torso and forelegs off the ground. It planned to crush him, and the sight of the steel shod hooves reminded Gilead that there were creatures stronger than him.

Maybe he could slit its throat.

"Not Montana," someone called, and the beast's master managed to enunciate, "Away."

With majestic slowness, the animal settled back into almost a seated position, as if it were some sort of giant dog. "Good, away," Joshua said forcefully. He struggled to his feet, which was difficult with one hand clutching at his painfully swelling jaw. The bruise was already livid on his pale, freckled skin. His red hair formed a sweat-streaked halo of fire around his face.

Gilead eyed the man doubtfully before offering his own hand to steady him. Joshua took it, and leaned on him. Gilead kept an eye on the other men, but one was shaking his head sadly, and another, whose yellow hair was thick and long, forming not just a halo but a whole corona, was staring rapt, the world's largest grin on his face.

The birds had stopped crying.

"Thank you," said Joshua, still clutching Gilead's arm, "for not killing my horse. He is my favorite."

"Sure," Gilead said. "I kind of thought it was going the other way around, truth be told." He still didn't trust any of them, and Joshua's command to the horse to stand down might have been more to preserve a pet than to save Gilead, but the sleeper beckoned the blond over.

The blond's large head of hair was one of the more amazing things Gilead had seen since waking on Nwwwlf. The man's hair sprang out in kinks and tight coils as if he were African. Gilead remembered no Africans amongst the settlers he saw before going under. Maybe there'd been a few.

"Can you take care of him?" he asked.

"Absolutely not," the blond said. "You spared his life, he's your responsibility."

"Hank," Joshua grated in warning tones.

"Would you like me to carry you?" Hank was as tall as Gilead, and could easily have lifted even so solid a man as Joshua. Joshua wasn't much shorter, but lacked Hank's bulk.

"I would like you to get me on my horse and follow me back," Joshua said. "I would then like you to find me some ice."

"You'll be needing that," Gilead agreed affably.

The men had their horses on the other side of the grove, and the lanky one who had been shaking his head sadly went and got them. He seemed the most sober of the lot, clothed in a dark brown tunic and a long, dark brown vest. Joshua was in green, and Hank wore red. They were a festive bunch, merry men all.

Joshua looked at Gilead as the horses appeared. Gilead knew he looked strange to them. He wore lightweight workout clothes which might last until the sun went nova, and the lines were both more tailored than the clothing of Nwwwlf, but looser. They suited his athletic frame and were comfortable. He had been stylish centuries ago, in his new civilian clothes.

"You don't seem dressed for riding," Joshua said. For someone whose face was turning a livid black and purple, he seemed remarkably cheerful.

Gilead smiled, and kept it pleasant. He wasn't the one with a bruised jaw. He had tried hard not to break it, and the lack of screaming suggested he'd succeeded. "I ran."

"Will you be running back? I have no mount to offer you, and you look tired."

Gilead smiled again. "I'm not."

Joshua laughed and winced, and one of the others snorted. "It's true about you," Hank said. "You're like the Pan."

"I am not. I don't have the horns." He ran his hands through his dark hair, lifting it to show not the smallest bud of the horns the Pan sported.

Joshua leaned from his horse as if inspecting Gilead's scalp. "Still, I feel no qualms about allowing you to walk—or run—back to the palace. Do come see me. I would take it amiss if you did not inquire after my welfare."

"I am deeply concerned for your welfare," Gilead said. "I will be sure to stop by."

The ridiculous encounter occupied Gilead's mind for the remainder of his run. It was a relief, almost being crushed by a horse, and the change in scene for the swordplay made him feel almost human. He found himself checking out the birds, trying to figure if they were actually birds, but thought they weren't.

His valet waited for him at the palace. The boy looked frightened.

"What's the matter," Gilead asked. He began shedding clothes, somewhat like a snake shed its skin. The clothes were soaked in sweat, but Teth picked them up as they fell. It was weird, having the kid follow him around and look after his stuff. But there were no machines. Gilead missed the machines, and wanted them back. Maybe he could become an industrialist, and make lots of stuff and lots of money. People would love it.

"They are saying you fought Sir Joshua. He is the king's champion."

It made Gilead crazy that someone had thought it a good idea to use archaic titles of nobility. That someone must have run roughshod over the other settlers to impose this misbegotten fantasy on them.

"We had a friendly match-up. It wasn't a big deal."

He went into the bathing room. The tub was full of warm water. There were advantages to a valet. Teth followed him. There were also disadvantages.

Teth still clutched the sodden workout clothes. "But is he angry?"

Gilead settled happily into the tub. He was very sore on his right side. He could only imagine how he would have felt if he'd had to stab the plunging horse. He continued to have trouble with the physics of that one. "Nah. He started it, after all."

Teth stared wide-eyed, and Gilead realized the boy wanted to know what had happened. He reached for the soap, there being no shampoo, and said, "You want me to tell you about it?"

Teth nodded.

"Put down the clothes and take a seat," Gilead said.

The bath and talking to the boy did him some good. He stood on his balcony staring down into the practice yard, working on not thinking about Andrea. He would have to do something with his life. He knew that, but it was hard to care. He had no real interest in working for the king. It was pretty obvious, however, that no one thought he had a choice in the matter.

But he did have a choice, and he knew it. He had started to ask more questions about the geography of the place under the guise of understanding the Pan and their strategic position. Really, he wanted to know if there were other human settlements outside of the Landing's reach where he could take the sleepers. No one mentioned such settlements, and part of him didn't want to give his game away by asking questions that were too obvious, and part of him just didn't care.

Officially, no one left First Landing's valley. Unofficially, some did, but the consensus view was that they died. Wild animals, lack of support, and, most importantly, lack of Earth bugs, made them weak, their children puny, and their wives ugly. It was a well-known fact. Urban myth, clever propaganda, or God's own truth, it was the story.

Gilead had read enough manuals and could always kidnap McCrary. He just needed to learn enough to have a place to take everyone. Most weren't soldiers, and he couldn't count on their stamina.

Gilead knew he didn't have an army, and taking Fort Stampo would require more than one man and an old doctor. He shrugged and contented himself with putting it off for the future. Right now, he had to visit Mr. Calhoun.

When Gilead found Joshua Calhoun, he was clean if not lovely. Gilead revised his estimate of the man's age up to thirty or thereabouts. His wild eyes and red hair, his sunburn and freckles, made him look younger, but he had the solidity that came with full growth and density. He was lightly clad in breeches and a thin shirt. He had no extra body fat, but was not scrawny. Far from it. Gilead wondered who his ancestors were and whether he had known them. He didn't look like Mason or Llew, but you never knew.

"How are you doing, Mr. Calhoun?" he asked. It was a worthwhile question. The swelling on the redhead's face was ugly.

"I am fine, sleeper," Joshua said, his speech a little thick. He held a bag of lumps that had to be ice against his face. "But I have no inclination to face you again anytime soon."

Gilead smiled, his unmarked face and strong bones a stark contrast with Joshua's puffed swelling. "Likewise, I'm sure. I thought you were planning to kill me."

Joshua snorted, and then looked pained. "That would have been wasteful. One must test one's rivals."

He gestured to a rush chair, and Gilead sat in it. "I am not your rival," Gilead said.

"You've been training as if you are," Joshua said. He moved the bag farther up his jaw, and touched the spot tenderly with his other hand. "It gets very cold," he pointed out.

"I've been training," Gilead said.

"Why, if you are not my rival?" Joshua asked.

It helped him not to think. He didn't say that out loud. "I don't have anything else to do. My wife and friends are gone."

Joshua gave him a quick look at the mention of his wife, but only said, "You need to train with me and my comrades."

Gilead gave him the evil eye. "I don't know that you've shown I need to do that."

Joshua's eyes, which were a very pale brown, sparked with fire. "Perhaps we need to train with you. You could be more polite about it."

Gilead laughed. "I don't see that either. And I'm not being polite."

"Don't be difficult. You can start by coming to dinner tonight." He moved the bag of ice again.

CHAPTER 6

GILEAD'S TRAINING CONTINUED. HE NO longer faced grim opponents who worked him hard but had some slight fear of killing him. Now, he faced a group of maniacs who thought him invulnerable. By day they tried to kill him. At night they quizzed him relentlessly on all his enhancements. The part of him that continued to mull over how to rescue the other sleepers cautioned against sharing too much information, but this led to repeated tests, that he worried would ultimately kill him. He explained that he was not superhuman, just as good as any Olympic athlete could be, and maybe, which he didn't mention, just a little better. They liked the idea of the Olympics, and spent several evenings addressing the advisability of importing them to Nwwwlf.

The beer in the evenings had its own benefits, and for several nights he slept soundly. At some point, however, the part of him that only waited for a little healing to happen before it kicked back in, brought the dreams back. The nightmares were no longer of Andrea in a casket. Now, Mason and Llew and others he couldn't see very well gasped for air in boxes buried underground, or screamed as they were sent, boxed, into a furnace for premature cremation.

One evening, as he assured Hank and his head of yellow hair—which was almost a separate person—that no, he couldn't stop a musket ball, yes, fire would burn him, and, no, he couldn't breathe water, Joshua leaned across the table, his eyes intent.

The palace had several kitchens and even more dining halls. When the king dined in private or with only select invitees, the other inhabitants were removed to their own halls. Joshua had a family, apparently, but he spent many of his dinners with his men. This dining hall was not far from the practice yard, and very close to the kitchen. The food was always hot, and there was plenty of it. The beer was weaker than what Gilead thought right, but there was plenty of that as well.

Joshua's pale brown eyes glowed like gold in the candlelight. His face had returned to normal, and was hard and solid again. "Gilead," he said softly, but in tones audible to all at the table, "are you ready for our match?"

Gilead stopped with his fork halfway to his mouth. He was eating his eggs. If you didn't eat eggs from Earth chickens at least once a day, you languished and got feeble. Some people died. Fortunately, the egg supply was plentiful, at least in the palace. "What match? We've had many matches."

"If you are to be my successor, you must prove yourself worthy by besting me in combat." Joshua raised his goblet in a toast to Gilead.

"Doesn't our first match count for that?" Gilead asked.

"That was just a test," Hank said helpfully. "We wanted to see if you were worth our trouble."

"Like a job interview," Gilead offered, also helpfully. He stretched his arms high over his head before dropping them clasped at the base of his skull. "What if I don't want the job?" He had been afraid he was stuck with his "championship" already. It was nice to have a possible out.

"It is a great honor," Joshua said. "You must not treat it lightly."

"I don't know that it fits with my career goals," Gilead said.

"Gilead," Joshua said in warning. He stopped, scowling.

Gilead remained silent, and then relented. "How about you give me the job description? You don't seem to be the king's bodyguard."

"Only in battle," Joshua replied. "Then I am always at his side."

"Are any battles coming up?" It seemed like a good thing to know.

"In the summer we march against the Pan." The year was slightly longer than Earth's, but summer was approaching. The growing seasons were long, but so were the winters.

"I never met a lot of Pan," Gilead said, "but I never had any quarrel with them."

"They are kidnappers," Hank pointed out. "They steal our children."

"And our crops," Joshua said. "They raid, and they kill, and they rob."

"And what do you all do to them?" Gilead asked.

"We destroy their nests," Hank said with grim satisfaction. The yellow hair nodded with him.

"Damn," Gilead said. "They're people, too. They came here just like your ancestors did, to find new land and build a world. It's huge here." McCrary's lab had held photos from orbit. Somewhat like Earth's Europe and Asia but bigger, a huge land mass sprawled across a large portion of the northern hemisphere, leaving just enough room for a good bit of ocean before the other land mass spanning the northern and southern hemispheres bifurcated the globe. Something the size of Australia sat all lonely to the south of the Eurasia analog. The settlers had picked the bifurcating mass for landing. "Why don't you just leave each other alone? It's like you're fighting over one valley in North Carolina."

"I do not know North Carolina," Joshua said dismissively.

Gilead pounced. "And that's sad, you know? Here you have this massive kidnapping program yourselves, where you keep people who you've never met in a sleep close to death for centuries—which can't be good for them—and wake them up once every fifty years, all in the name of preserving your heritage, and you don't know where North Carolina is?"

"I'd wager," Hank said loftily, "that it's on Earth." He poured himself more beer.

"Very good," Gilead assured him. An evil demon possessed him. "You know, I think I've figured out what I want to do with my life, seeing as how I'm stuck here. I'll set up as a school teacher. Dr. McCrary is resuscitating the medical arts. I'll teach science, maybe work on some history, develop some basic machinery, work on the wheel—I miss the wheel—and plumbing. It'll be a trade school with civics and science. All brought straight from Earth via a very long detour."

"You want to be a school teacher?" Ignoring the insult about the wheel, Joshua focused on the more horrific issue.

Gilead nodded enthusiastically. It had only just occurred to him, but the idea was growing on him. "I've been a soldier. I came here with my wife to build, not to fight."

Hank was equally appalled, and the other men around the table looked embarrassed for Gilead. They didn't always talk a lot, but they knew well enough when someone was blowing interesting job opportunities. Hank asked, "Where is the glory in that?"

Gilead's closest friend had died at his side not

two years earlier, blown to kingdom come by shock grenade. "I found no glory in fighting," he said. "Just a lot of death."

"You can't do that," Joshua said. "You are to be the king's champion. He will have a soldier from the stars, from our own past, to protect him, to help him win." He spoke with almost religious fervor. For such a solid man, with such very red hair, to sound so convinced of the manifest destiny of it all gave Gilead a moment of unease. It wasn't just their ancestors and leaders who were crazy. They were all a bunch of aliens to him. He should try and remember that.

"I'm just a guy," Gilead said.

"You are enhanced," Hank said.

"You beat me yesterday," Gilead pointed out.

Hank shrugged this off. "You are still learning the sword. You bested Joshua on first meeting. You will likely do so again."

"And we must fight," Joshua said earnestly. "The king must have the best champion."

Finally curious, Gilead asked, "How would we fight?" There had been no jousting so far.

Joshua's eyes were intense, molten, the eyes of a crazy person. "To the death, of course."

Gilead was on his feet, swearing with great force, velocity, and sincerity. When he ran down, he simply said, "No. I am not going to fight to the death for a job interview. I'm going back to Stampo, and they can put me back in the sleeping quarters." He had no such intention, but maybe he could escape into the wilds, evade the evil Pan, and set up as a hermit over in the Tennessee analog. Other people had to have left this loony bin.

This was greeted with resounding silence. It lasted for several seconds before his dining companions broke into hysterical laughter. Hank and Willem, who was otherwise a quiet man, both expelled beer through their noses.

Gilead sat back down in disgust.

"That was very amazing swearing," Hank said admiringly. "I am glad we are preserving our Earth heritage with you."

"Perhaps you could teach it in your new school," Joshua suggested.

Willem took another swallow of beer. "It would be so wasteful. I cannot fathom how you believed him."

Gilead leaned closer to him. "Because I think you're all crazy, that's why."

"I am insulted, but I forgive you," Willem said in a very dignified way. He poured more beer into Gilead's goblet.

They all forgave each other, and Gilead learned that the championship bout would take place over several days, with much in the way of merriment and shenanigans, feasting and fun, and games of skill and chance. There was a long discussion over whether there would be jesters, and whether jesters were jugglers, and whether Gilead knew the meaning of either word, but, finally, the kitchen refused to provide more beer, and they attempted to stand. Gilead and Joshua succeeded, and reached the hall. It was part of the new construction, and consisted of large oaken beams and rough plaster walls. The floors rustled with dried grasses.

"My friend," Joshua said, "may I ask you a question?"

"Indeed, you may," Gilead replied. He kept his speech deliberate. "I will even answer it if I can."

"You spoke of a wife earlier?"

Gilead sighed, and his heart broke a little all over again. It would be best not to weep. Not here. "I did."

"Is she still sleeping?" Joshua asked.

"No, my friend. She died long ago." They reached

the stairs, and Gilead took his leave, keeping his steps deliberate so no one could say he ran.

The king's young cousin had requested an audience. Because Lord Arran McDev was a cousin and managed the sleeper and his household, the king's secretary had granted the scholarly young man his request. Cleverly, the secretary set the interview for a mere thirty minutes before the king heard cases, so that whatever troubles the cousin brought with him, the time would be limited.

The king appreciated his secretary, and relied upon him to think like this. Nonetheless, he smiled broadly at Arran, who looked markedly better than he had when Clarence had first sent him to Stampo as an overly bookish young man who needed more sunshine and responsibilities. He had grown into them, it appeared.

Arran himself was very glad. He had gotten through what could have been an incredibly difficult scene with the sleeper and the queen, and there appeared to be no talk of Gilead's reaction to her at the court. He might prefer his studies of the physical world, but he had grown up in the court, and knew well that the king could replace him as apprentice to the older sleeper and minder of the new one. He was learning too much to surrender his roles happily.

Clarence was kind, as he always was with Arran, but although he inquired after Arran's father and siblings, his thoughts on the new sleeper, and how the doctor fared, he never once inquired as to the reason for Arran's visit. This made Arran uncomfortable, as the secretary had made sure he knew of Clarence's other obligations for the afternoon.

Arran had done his best to frame his proposal as something that would lead to the greatest good for the greatest number of people, the sleepers included, but he needed time to present it properly.

The anteroom leading to the chamber that served as a court was intimate, large enough for only a desk and three chairs. Clarence had not seated himself behind the desk, but taken, more informally, one of the two freestanding chairs. They were large and comfortable.

Clarence's clear blue eyes were alive with laughter when he finally said, "Should I ask you why you have come to see me, cousin? You appear to have something on your mind."

Arran was acutely aware that he only had ten minutes to share it, and his carefully rehearsed speech abandoned him. He had planned a Socratic approach, with leading questions designed to show Clarence how much he could get by waking the sleepers. He didn't think ten minutes was long enough for all that and a discussion, too. "I have an idea I hope you will like," he blurted out. "I am asking you to consider waking all the sleepers."

Clarence's very pale eyebrows shot up. "I cannot do that, cousin. I am sorry."

Arran rushed on. "It has been very amazing, working with the two sleepers. I have learned so much from Robert, but that is to be expected since he is a doctor and a man of science. What is more incredible is that the soldier is also highly educated. Clearly, in our past, even soldiers understood technology and science. Everyone had a basic understanding of how the world worked. We could have that again, but we should awaken the people who know these things. If even the soldiers are educated—" He paused for breath, beaming, but his smile faded as he saw the look in Clarence's eyes. Perhaps he should not have made so clear his opinion of the intelligence of the king's warriors. He couldn't stop now. "Then there is a vast supply of knowledge that the sleepers can provide us. We would have enough learning, enough experts, to—" He stopped again, groping for the right word.

"Lay a foundation?" Clarence offered helpfully.

Arran nodded, and scooted to the edge of his seat. He stared earnestly at the golden face and the crystalline eyes. "Yes. Exactly. To lay a good foundation for so many people to become educated, and perhaps we could rebuild our past. We could have electricity and medicines and horseless carts. It would be for the greater good."

"We cannot be so selfish, Arran," Clarence said and rose to his feet. "It was decided long ago what the greatest good is. And the greatest good includes our descendants who must also benefit from the sleeper legacy." The king nodded at his secretary, who had appeared silently in the doorway with a black robe draped over his left arm. "We must not forget them in a rush to have these imaginary luxuries of yours."

Clarence took the robe and swirled it over his shoulders as if the sober garment were a cape. "Come. Join me in the court. You will find it interesting. Educational even."

There would be no further discussion, Arran knew. He felt a slight shame, and realized it was because he had forgotten to mention the interests of those who could not speak for themselves, namely, the unconscious sleepers. Instead, he had dwelt upon his own reasons for wanting them awakened. He felt as if Gilead would not have approved, and this annoyed him. It was very difficult to ever be annoyed with Clarence. It was much easier to be annoyed with Gilead for causing him, even if Gilead did not know it, to come up with these harebrained notions.

Unhappily, he followed Clarence into the courtroom, where the king ascended to a raised dais behind a judge's bench over two meters in length. Wooden seating held a couple dozen people who looked like farmers, and several more who wore the king's colors. Arran had no idea why they were there or what they wanted. The ones in farmers' smocks did not look like petitioners but like prisoners, even their wives and children.

They rose to their feet at the king's entrance, and did not sit until he did. The secretary motioned Arran toward the benches, but they were full, and he propped himself with his shoulders against the wall. He folded his arms. He was not a soldier to stand at attention.

Arran looked down at the older man in the end seat next to where he stood. It was Dr. McCrary. Maybe his presence meant the session actually would be educational, but his eyes were sad and hunted.

The prosecutor approached the bench. He, too, wore black robes like those of the king. His brown hair, speckled grey, hung in a long braid down his back, and he was round and well fed. He read the charges. The farmers had attempted to leave the valley and head into the wilderness with their families and their cattle, their wagons loaded with the winter's crops and all their worldly possessions. The prosecutor charged the three men and their families with desertion and treason.

Looking across the room, Arran saw one of the men try to stand. The soldier next to him shoved him back down. A girl sobbed and turned her face into the shoulder of a woman, likely her mother, at her side. The adult woman's face was set and grim.

"How do you plead?" Clarence asked. His face was a cold mask, stiff and haughty. He could not like it when his subjects tried to abandon him. His subjects liked being caught even less, and another of the children started to cry.

Arran felt a tightness in his throat, and he realized he was trembling. He felt a tugging at his sleeve.

His face grim, McCrary said, "Sit down, son." He scooted down the bench as far as he could, and left a small, cleared spot, into which Arran gratefully dropped.

Under cover of the sobbing, Arran whispered, "What are you doing here?"

"I like to come watch justice at work," Robert said. He kept his eyes fixed on the king.

"What happens next?" Arran asked.

"They don't consult me," the older man said, "but I've seen enough of these. I can guess."

"Tell me," Arran forced himself to say. He didn't want to know. He didn't want to stay, and he wanted the vise around his throat to let go.

"He will find them guilty. These folks can never afford a lawyer and no one wants to represent a bunch of deserters. Their punishment will be the mines, the toadfat farms, or the palace kitchen. This will depend more on where he needs the labor than on the severity of the crime. Just watch. It's very educational."

Arran swallowed, spooked that Dr. McCrary's admonition mirrored the guidance Clarence had given him. He was more spooked that a part of him believed the older man. Had he not been standing in the court room himself, watching Clarence's implacable countenance and the haunted terror on the faces of the farmers, he would have sworn that Clarence would never do such a thing. He knew leaving was disfavored, and the occasional news of a vanished family was told in whispers, but he had not known it counted as treason. Perhaps, only if one were caught.

As McCrary had predicted, there was no counsel for the defense.

The prosecutor called one of the soldiers to a large chair near the king. The soldier swore to tell the truth, and the prosecutor asked him to say who he was and describe what he had seen two weeks earlier, when he had caught these families in the act.

The soldier obliged, volunteering that it had upset him greatly, what they were doing. He and his squad were stationed in Faraway, in the northeast where the Pan preyed. He and three men had been patrolling the roads north of the town, when they had heard the oxen. The oxen weren't happy with what was being asked of them, them being natural beasts.

This baffled the prosecutor, but only momentarily, and he stopped himself, with obvious effort from inquiring into the relevance of the oxen's preferences. Had anyone asked him, Arran could have told him that the centuries of human presence in Landing had transformed it into a highly habitable environment for humans and other Earth mammals, and that the beasts could smell the difference. They would be the ones asked to transform the subtly unattractive new grasses into meat and milk for the humans. The soldier was likely not wrong in his estimation of the oxen's desires.

"What did you see?" the prosecutor asked.

"Them," the soldier pointed. "Those three men and all their families."

The prosecutor rattled off three names, and told them to stand. Three men in their early thirties rose to their feet. One looked stunned, and another grim, but the third, a blond man with lots of fine yellow hair, looked slowly around the room, his steady gaze an accusation against all who held him there. A large bruise discolored one side of his neck and reached livid fingers up his jaw. Arran was no soldier, but it looked to him like it came from a knockout blow.

"These were the men you saw?" the prosecutor asked. When the soldier nodded, the prosecutor pointed at them with his own plump hand and waved the men back to their seats.

"What else did you see?"

"What you said earlier. Each family had two wagons, and they were full. They had everything they could possibly own in them—bedding, pans, and tons of food. All those children, they were there, too."

The prosecutor pursed his full lips. "What did you make of all that?"

The soldier look vaguely astonished at the stupidity of the question. "It was obvious. They were deserting the valley."

The squad had ordered the families back, only to find themselves ignored. This frustrated the squad leader no end, and he had been forced to threaten to shoot. He had a good archer with him, and it would all have gone as it should have had not one of the farmers stabbed the archer's horse with a pitchfork, and knocked the archer out with the other end of it.

The prosecutor was shocked. "He attacked the king's men? Which one?"

The witness pointed at the man who had surveyed the room earlier. Arran was not surprised. The rangy farmer didn't look like he would take anything lying down, and there were the bruises.

"And his horse," the soldier reminded the prosecutor.

A lengthy description ensued of the return to Faraway, the subsequent incarceration of all involved, which had been difficult given the numbers and children, and, then, finally, the journey to First Landing for a trial before the king.

The soldier finally finished his testimony and stood down. The prosecutor sat, too, well satisfied.

One of the clerks poured the king a drink. The fluid was thick, and looked like yoghurt. Arran's stomach rumbled. McCrary gave him a poke with his elbow.

Refreshed, the king turned to the motley assemblage. "Do any of you wish to speak?"

The bruised man stood. "Is there any reason to? A king who will not let us leave will surely not let us defend ourselves."

Clarence frowned, and his beautiful face also looked sad. "Of course, you may speak. But be careful that what you say doesn't make your situation worse."

A laugh escaped the man's lips. "I don't see what could make our situation worse."

Arran stretched very tall, to see the others, wishing he had remained standing. The man's wife had a very stiff back, but her arms were around two of her children, and she might have been trembling.

The man continued scanning the audience as if looking to meet someone's eyes. He stared hard at the doctor at one point, and McCrary finally looked away. He could offer no help. Arran realized that he could not either.

"The king's men took our farms and flooded them for the king's toadfats," the farmer said.

Arran had heard talk of an oil shortage. The taking must have been a response to that problem.

The prosecutor couldn't stop himself from interrupting. "Did you seek assistance from your township?"

"The king's mayor told us we could work on someone else's land. Or the king's."

"Then why did you leave?" the lawyer asked, as if curious.

"We wanted our own land, like we had before."

Arran furtively checked Clarence's face throughout the exchange. He kept waiting for the king to explain how the decision was necessary for the greater good. But Clarence appeared to feel no need to defend himself. It didn't seem fair.

"One can't always have everything one wants," the prosecutor said, and sniffed.

"The king can," the farmer observed.

"That's enough," Clarence said. "It is time for your sentencing."

"By your leave, sire," Arran said. He had no memory of rising to his feet. Nor was he certain what it was he meant to say now that he had the king's attention.

Clarence looked at him quizzically, and his eyes softened. He was no longer the harsh judge but the concerned older cousin. Arran wasn't fooled. He could see now whom he faced, and a chill circled his body somewhere around his ribs.

"No, lad," the farmer said. "You sit down." He looked to McCrary again, but McCrary stared straight ahead.

"You would be wise to take the man's advice," Clarence suggested. His voice was not menacing, but soft and gentle.

"I was going to suggest," Arran said quickly, "that there is room for them at Fort Stampo." Stampo was the king's property, and it was better than the mines. Anything had to be better than the mines, and Arran had a sick certainty that these families would be sent there where they would die of hunger, a rockfall, or the simple lack of sun. "There is always a need for help in the kitchen and the stables. There are kitchen gardens."

The farmer looked both bemused and disdainful, a strange combination on a stranger's face.

Clarence eyed the men, his gaze lingering over each of them, finally settling on the ringleader. He took his time returning his attention to Arran. "It's a generous offer, cousin. But I don't think the object of your charity appreciates it." He gave Arran a chilly smile, and Arran knew with utter certainty that Clarence didn't mean that smile. He had never seen this side of the king, and he was astonished how much he disliked it.

"Please," Arran said. His face was hot, but he didn't care—anything to make the vise around his throat go away. He could beg where the farmer couldn't.

"Arran," Clarence said, and he no longer wore the cousinly smile. "That is enough." He turned back to the rebel farmers. "The women and children will go to Stampo. The men will go to the mines."

The farm families did not take their sentencing well.

The king invited a small group of fifty persons to dine with him. The hall was elaborate with plaster walls smoothed by long-dead machines, and now covered by tapestries depicting the history of humanity on Nwwwlf. One started to the left of the entry door, where a sky of darkest indigo held stars, with the largest front and center. Nwwwlf's sun, the source of light and energy, held a position of honor. It looked like a nice, yellow G type star.

Floating before it was a globe, Earth-like in its colors, with only the slightest hint of its greens edging toward lime. Cloud cover blanketed the Eurasia analog, visible in part at the edge of the globe, but the continent that might have been a unified Western Hemisphere, also held pride of place toward the front. A small star showed several hundred kilometers inland from the eastern seaboard. A speck of shining metal, not to scale, orbited the planet, its trajectory limned by dashed lines around the globe.

The next tapestry was ground-based, a vista from a jungle looking heavenward at a fleet of machines, as if all the shuttles of the starship had come in at once. Gilead took that as poetic license, but he wondered.

In the same tapestry, but inset as a separate panel, as if meant to show a scene contemporaneous to the shuttle landing, the weaving showed an aerial view of the spot along the river where Landing stood now. There was meadow before the expanse of trees, as if flooding took place with some regularity. The volume of trees had been depleted since the tapestry was made, as Gilead knew from his explorations. Then the building began on the adjacent panel. Excavators and earthmovers, machines the size of small houses, were brought down to the planet to build large structures to house them all.

He recognized the clothing in the next one. It matched what he thought right and proper, but several wore a red cross on their coats, as if there had been sickness. Looking closer, he saw that some of the inhabitants were Pan. The rift had not been immediate.

Turning to the next tapestry, he found his path blocked by two young women in party clothes. Their full skirts fell almost to their ankles, and their silken corsets—or whatever those tight things they wore around their breasts were called—fell almost to their nipples. He pulled his eyes up quickly, and they giggled, the dark haired one managing a blush. He nodded, unsmiling and uninterested.

He felt a hand on his shoulder, and turned to find Robert McCrary. "Be careful," the doctor cautioned, pulling him away from the women. "You sleep with one of these women and you have to marry her. And, they can all get pregnant. With your looks and fame you need to watch it. The word is a lot of them would be happy to land you."

Gilead knew about the lack of contraceptives. The implications were breathtaking, and explained a lot, but he literally couldn't imagine Andrea's reaction to this state of affairs. He merely, nodded, however, and waited.

The bearded old doctor looked at him with some

apprehension. "At least you don't have to take a knee this time," McCrary said.

Although he had not planned to in any event, Gilead was relieved not to be drawing attention to himself.

McCrary drew a large breath, and had the look of a man intent on saying something, if not important, very meaningful. "Are you planning to return to Stampo?" McCrary asked quietly and rapidly, his Nwwwlf intonations absent from his speech, as if to make it harder for any listeners to understand.

Gilead felt himself grow very still, and he could hear his breath inside his body. He did not need this man questioning him. He made sure that his reply had no tone. "Why should I?"

"Don't play dumb with me, soldier. I know you want to wake everyone up. Despite your wife."

Again, Gilead struggled to keep his voice even. "What about my wife?"

McCrary's brows shot up, as if in surprise. McCrary had certainly implied that he knew the significance to Gilead of the queen's looks. Gilead had not pursued the issue with him at the time. "You know what I mean. Arran told me what happened with you—how you mistook the queen for her. Arran thinks that you think your wife is long dead."

"Have you been gossiping with anyone else, old man?" His voice shook.

"I'm sorry. I'm sorry, Gilead. I should not have mentioned your wife."

Gilead lifted a hand, and made a warding motion.

McCrary eyed him bleakly. "But I'm sure you haven't forgotten the others."

Gilead didn't really trust the old man. McCrary was someone who could have done a great deal to get people out. The doctor had had his reasons not to, but it was still very wrong. "My incentives changed when I learned of Andrea's death," Gilead said coldly. He felt no need to share his plans. And, McCrary had a threat hanging over his family, which meant he'd likely take any information straight to the king.

"You know that the person I tried to wake before you didn't make it," McCrary said. He seemed to be struggling to say something, and finally spoke very quietly, "I am worried that they've been in there too long."

Gilead shrugged. "Tell the king."

"I did," McCrary hissed. "He told me not to worry about it. The people would never accept 'squandering their heritage.'" He enunciated the last few words in a pedantic singsong, in obvious mockery of whomever he mimicked.

"He should explain it to them. It's not complicated. You're a doctor. Someone died. Wake 'em all up. End of story."

McCrary looked exasperated. "I don't think you understand how things are around here."

"No," Gilead agreed. "I don't." What McCrary had said was very logical, but he suspected the older man of trying to trap him somehow. Perhaps whoever had a hold over the doctor's family wanted to acquire one over Gilead.

"It's like a religious thing for them," McCrary began, but Gilead stopped him.

"I'm sorry. I am not interested in the strange beliefs of these people." The beliefs were the product of some person who had been in the starship who had imposed a whole lot of idiocy on a set of gullible fools, who had passed it down to their children. He hated whoever had woken Andrea and not him. He almost hated Andrea for having children with someone else. He was furious at her for leaving him, and he was furious at her for being dead. He could be irrational, too.

McCrary was visibly angry. "You might be more interested in your comrades."

Gilead closed his eyes. He must not trust this man. He had already told Gilead he was compromised. "Do you have someone in there?"

He waited for the answer, watching the play of emotion on McCrary's face. "No," he said, obviously lying. McCrary trusted Gilead no more than Gilead trusted him.

Gilead walked away from the doctor.

He saw a familiar face, one he had grown accustomed to seeing regularly. Behind him milled other familiar men, all invited to the king's feast. They were all knights, Joshua had explained in passing, as if it were natural for a grown man to lay claim to that title when his ancestors came from the Western Hemisphere, and—even worse—going by his name, North America.

"Hah," Joshua exclaimed. "There you are. The contest will be announced tonight." He stepped back and admired Gilead. "We are a handsome pair. You need to find a wife, you know. I've had maybe twenty maidens fair ask my wife to introduce you. It's getting tiring."

Gilead had no interest in another wife. He had other things to do. He noticed a woman peering from behind her large husband. As Joshua introduced his own wife, a woman of medium height with large green eyes and curls of dark gold, a trumpet sounded. Two people entered, wearing clothes of bright and happy colors, red and deep blue. Clarence, with his fine, golden hair, and red tunic, entered first. Something glinted on his head. It was a slim, golden band, almost a wire it was so slender. Very tasteful, Gilead thought acidly. Behind him came a woman with raven black hair, her lips painted red as blood, the dark lashes around her blue eyes creating a smoky effect with which Gilead was all too familiar.

This time, he was prepared, and noticed that she returned his gaze, assessing him just as much as he had appraised her. There was warmth in her eyes, but he forced himself to look away. There was only so much torture he could take. Perhaps he should kidnap the doctor right now, storm the fort, and wake up whoever was left. They could all leave together, go find a valley of their own.

Clarence was watching him, and his eyes were wary. Gilead stared back. This man wanted Gilead as a bodyguard, a status symbol, and as a possible soldier in his armies. He held no interest for Gilead.

The same was not true of the others in the room. All eyes were on the king. All squared shoulders faced him, and many was the face filled with happy gladness to see this man.

Dinner was announced, and the guests filled the two long trestle tables piled high with casseroles and roasts, beds of shimmering gelatin with berries buoyant inside them, tall flagons styled as swans, and, in the center of it all, a turkey restored to an uncanny resemblance of its life-like state. Bowls of colored eggs had their own places, too. Servants stood ready to pass and serve, and one came to Gilead's side to escort him to a place of honor next to the king.

This meant Gilead sat only two persons away from the queen and her painted red mouth, for the table was wide enough for Clarence and Mary to share its head. Joshua, the reigning champion, sat across from Gilead.

Gilead took care not to look at her, more for his own sake than to avoid disturbing the king. Clarence himself proved an easy dinner host. He inquired after Gilead's service and his impressions of other worlds, modestly describing himself as nowhere near as well travelled. His understanding of astronomy and faster than light travel was not poor, and he confessed to a liking for mathematics.

"I have long enjoyed the doctor's descriptions of Earth and its history," he said. "I try to understand how it might apply here."

This man, Gilead thought, was the one man who need not fear the king's censure. This man might answer his questions. He approached his topic obliquely. "There are many differences," Gilead said, "that make comparison difficult."

Clarence raised his brows and plucked a colored egg from the bowl in front of him. He tapped it on his plate and peeled it, leaving the bits of shell on the cloth that covered the table in a radiant blue, a blue that mirrored the color of the sky. "Why do you say that?"

"Your neighbors are not other people," Gilead said.

"True enough," the king agreed, confirming what Gilead had suspected of their view of the Pan.

"Although we, of course, thought of them as people. I had cousins who were born Pan."

He had shocked Clarence. "That cannot be," he said, leaving his egg momentarily forgotten on his plate.

"Yes," Gilead said, tapping his own pink egg. "It is true. It was very expensive for their parents, but they didn't think they could give one child all those advantages and not provide them for their siblings, too."

Gilead was close enough to see the pale golden eyebrows descend in a frown as the king cut his meat. "The parents were not Pan?" the king asked. "But they wanted their children to be?"

"You bet," Gilead said. "Didn't the doctor tell you?"

Clarence shot Gilead a look from the corner of his eyes. He was all about being amused again, a possible cover for whatever he truly thought and felt. "The doctor is afraid of me."

"I would imagine so," Gilead said.

The blue eyes lost their amusement. "Why is that?"

"The threat to his children?" Gilead said blandly.

The king stared at Gilead for many long seconds, as if it were terribly rude of Gilead to bring up threats to people's children. "To which particular threat," the king asked, "do you refer? I issue so many threats, so very many times a day, that it is sometimes hard for me to keep track." His voice was cold.

Gilead's egg was shelled. He chopped it fine with knife and fork. "Your historian told him his children would suffer terribly if he were to awaken any sleepers illegally." He scooped up the egg and dribbled it over something that looked like asparagus, which he liked.

"I wonder," the king mused, "how upset the doctor would be to learn that you told me of this?" He was looking amused again, almost mischievous. Gilead found it vaguely repellant. He felt a pang. Did the king not know of McCrary's children? Had he just made things worse for the doctor?

Mentally kicking himself, he made the mistake of looking in the queen's direction. She was talking to Joshua with great animation, and looked very lovely. He had the strangest sensation she knew he was watching her, and looked quickly away again.

The king was certainly watching him. "You admire the queen?" Clarence said.

Now he was in dangerous waters of his own. He cursed his weakness, he cursed his grief, and he very much wished that no one had heard him addressing her by his wife's name. "She is lovely, Clarence."

"Most people call me 'your grace' or 'sire,'" the king said absently. "Robert had difficulty with that as well, my father told me once. I suppose I shall have to be patient with you." He laid a hand over Gilead's wrist, and his grip was strong. The blue eyes were no longer amused but empty, as if vast bits of sky lay behind them. "How much does she resemble your wife?"

Here it was. The question allowed Gilead to study Mary. He wished he had greater strength of will. "Very much," he said. "Almost a twin."

He felt a great longing, so intense it was almost physical as it invaded his heart and his throat, stopping behind his eyes.

As he stared, another feeling crept over him, as if the reaction preceded the realization, and his stomach heaved, and he pushed his plate away. It took all the strength he could muster not to leave the room.

A woman was advised against pregnancy before entering the cold sleep. But Gilead and Andrea had planned to have children, and Andrea had taken the measures necessary to allow it. Usually those measures did not work right away, and Gilead had assumed this woman was not his own descendant, but what if she was? What if Andrea had already been pregnant when she woke?

The king leaned his chin in his hand and stared at Gilead's stricken face. "It's like watching a play," Clarence said confidingly, "but with no dialogue. Your feelings are all over the place. All the time. I shan't worry about treason with you."

For once, Gilead held his tongue. Telling this man anything had been a mistake. Telling him he might be his great grandfather-in-law cubed could be another. It wasn't as if he could demand a blood test, he told himself, but he looked down the table at McCrary and wondered. *Excuse me your royal highness, majesty, ma'am, but may I prick your finger? I need a drop of your blood and have this old spindle handy. Maybe*

Andrea and I had a child. He realized he hoped very much that they had.

"And now you are filled with bathos," the king said. He gestured to one of the attendants, who nodded and scurried off. Drapes at the other end of the room pulled back to reveal a stage perpendicular to the long tables. Musicians were seated in front of it. The stage itself had a set showing a forest glade, green and frondy, with three squabbling minstrels. It was a play, and it turned out, to everyone's eventual amusement, that one of the minstrels was a girl.

After the play, the merriment, the jugglers, and plenty of beer, the king stood, and everyone stopped talking. "Tonight," he declaimed, "I can tell you the games will commence on the first of June. I have decided the contestants for the role of king's champion, and they are numerous." He went on at length about how outstanding everyone had to be, not only in physical prowess, speed, and stamina, but in character, in honor, valor, and rectitude. His well-loved champion, Joshua Calhoun, was, of course, the first among equals. Joshua's virtues were extolled, and the dining hall filled with cheers. The king, without notes, Gilead was impressed to see, went through an entire roll call of fifteen names. All were greeted with applause, which grew more tepid toward the end.

When the king finally ran down, he raised his glass one last time to Gilead. "Last, but certainly not least, I commend to you all a newcomer in our midst, a sleeper from our own past, from humanity's planet of origin, Earth; a soldier, a star traveller, and now one of ours—Gilead Tan."

Everyone was tired of clapping, but they tried. It was late.

It was not so late that Gilead couldn't finally figure out where he stood. He had lost Andrea. Maybe he had gained some sort of great granddaughter, but he would probably never know the truth of it. He should, perhaps, be grateful that the old records were so hard to search. He had no hope of seeing his wife again, but he had friends still trapped in that mountain.

Gilead Tan had the lay of the land. He had met the players, learned the rules, and knew his real opponent. It wasn't Etienne, the king's thug from Stampo, or Joshua, the king's champion, but the king himself. Clarence was the living embodiment of the state, and was all powerful, owning the land, the law, and, functionally, the people in it. Gilead no longer faced mere duty. He faced a need. Gilead had to get his own people out, out of their sleep, and out of this valley.

Arran, his elbows on the large table, his hands clutching his dark hair, studied the chemistry books. They were old and kept under lock and key in the archives, but Dr. McCrary had access, and Arran, as his helper, did, too. He knew he studied the most basic form of organic chemistry, but the understanding had to start somewhere. He almost wished he could be put in the sleeping quarters and awaken in another five hundred years, long after all the lost science had been rediscovered.

He shook himself. He was lucky to have Robert McCrary to guide his studies and teach him practical applications. Earth had figured it all out without help. Nwwwlf could, too. Sometimes it hit him very hard, the lost legacy of his people. He wondered what decisions had been made that had led to their devolution, or whether it was just that life was so hard without the interstellar network of support. One thing was surely true about those long ago decisions, whatever Gilead might say and the doctor might think, the sleepers, their very existence, ensured that people continued to remember what they had lost, and what they might someday regain. He was very lucky that the king had seen his talents and sent him to Dr. McCrary. He thought of a young cousin who had not been so lucky. At least the lad was a decent shot.

He sat beneath a large glass window through which the yellow light of morning streamed. The type in the books was large and clear, very uniform and easy to read. Still, his mind returned to what he had witnessed the night before. It was better than thinking of the farmer's trial, which had absorbed him most of the day before.

The king had invited McCrary to his feast, but not Arran. Arran was a nobleman's fourth son, but he had no particular skill with a sword, certainly not any skill that set him even equal to those who attended the feast. Dr. McCrary was there because one always invited any sleeper in residence to anything. It added to the tone, and showed that one was cultured. Arran was just a scientist, and "scientist" was a word that few used other than Arran himself.

Instead, Arran had found himself first in the hallway, and then at the doorway to the tapestried dining hall. What was galling was that he stood there with other onlookers, forever an outsider to the warlike heart of governance. He had thought that Gilead had put soldiering behind him, particularly when the whole palace buzzed with the news that Gilead wanted to be a teacher. It didn't look to Arran like Gilead meant it, for there the newest sleeper had sat, at the king's right hand, talking, laughing, and catching the eye of the queen.

That would not do. Gilead may have been oblivious, but the breathless women angling for his attention, even just his field of view, were noted by the other men.

The king didn't seem to notice the queen's constant glances. Gilead played a dangerous game, but Arran wasn't sure that Gilead knew it.

To Arran, Gilead had presented himself as a man who had put war behind him, who had served his king and country, and had wanted to reap the rewards of that hard service with his wife on a new world. Arran had caught Gilead studying McCrary's manuals more than once, as if Gilead believed that he could understand and employ them. He was from a different world, where many people were educated enough to believe they could follow a manual. Gilead was not like Joshua and the men who surrounded him. They had their own learning and skills, but it all revolved around the sword and combat. Arran's learning they disdained.

At bottom, Arran was disappointed in Gilead. Gilead had been intent on waking all the sleepers. With his wife clearly no longer amongst them, Gilead had given up and now joined the warrior class.

Arran turned a page, and then turned it back. He had taken no notes, and remembered nothing. He and Dr. McCrary should return to the mountain keep and tend their sleeping patients. Arran felt a vague guilt about them, as if Gilead had infected him with his outrage, recovered, and left Arran the only one still suffering the malady. When the first sleeper turned out to be dead, Arran had, of course, started worrying about the physical viability of the others. That made sense. No one wanted them to die, and not just because they were Nwwwlf's heritage.

But now Arran had started to feel guilt over the fact that they were kept sleeping without their consent. They all had believed they would be awakened when they arrived at their destination.

They hadn't, of course, arrived at their destination. Arran lips twitched. It was a lawyerly observation and just the sort of observation that had earned him a cuff on the side of the head when he made similar points to his father. Arran had no interest in the law. It was just another form of combat. Or manipulation.

He wished Gilead would do something about the sleepers. There wasn't anything the soldier could do, of course. The sleepers were all hidden, the labs locked, and Gilead likely would never be allowed near them again.

He sighed and closed the book. He wrapped it carefully in its protective cloth and returned it to the librarian for safekeeping. He gathered his notes and went searching for the doctor.

CHAPTER 7

"EVEN IF I WANTED TO help you—which I don't—there is no way for me to do what you want." Gilead stared at two men, recovering his breath from the hard run he'd pushed himself to.

It was almost two weeks after the king's dinner and the last day of May. The tournament was the next day. His habits were well known apparently. Robert and Arran had waited for him in the park. He doubted they knew it, but it was the same spot where Joshua had ambushed him. The days were growing warmer, so the air was a little thicker, but the dappled shade across the grassy clearing and their intent faces were familiar.

Unlike their predecessors, the doctor and his assistant were unarmed, but they both shared their concern to good effect. Robert was stubborn. "You are a tactician. I don't even have to look at your chart to know that. You should be able to figure something out."

I've figured I won't trust you, is what I've figured, he thought. "It's guarded. The sleepers are hidden. I couldn't find them." Gilead paused for breath.

Both men scowled at him over this obvious lie, Arran's green eyes stern in his pale face.

Gilead, sweating hard from running, wiped a sleeve across his forehead and eyes. "More importantly, how would I get back there?"

Neither said anything, Robert just scowling at him through all his grey facial hair and Arran continuing to stare with those guilt-inducing green eyes. Lots of people had green eyes on Nwwwlf, but they were still unsettling.

Finally, Arran said, "We think it's your job to figure that out."

Now it was Gilead's turn to fix someone with a steely gaze, and he said to Robert, "But you can't come and help, can you?"

To his surprise, Robert turned an unhealthy shade of red. "I'm heading back," he said to Arran. "You can tell him." He nodded to Gilead and stomped off, an older man going on a long walk, and too agitated to keep his dignity.

The air on Gilead's wet skin was starting to cool him. Soon he would be cold. He folded his arms across his chest. "Is there something I need to know?"

Arran's face no longer wore the look of stern accusation. He looked away toward the trees, and then at the ground. "Robert lied to you."

"About what?" Gilead asked after a long pause. The trees had leafed out, and they fully obscured the sky, but the light that filtered through was still alien, still lime colored, as if some mineral with refractive powers floated weightless in the air.

Arran took a deep breath and looked up from whatever he'd been staring at on the ground. "Robert doesn't have a family. He told me he made all that up because you were so upset about your wife, and he felt guilty."

"Damn," Gilead said softly. Maybe the king had gone and had a talk with the doctor, laughed at him perhaps.

"He had trouble facing you. I think he tried long ago to wake the others up, but he failed." Arran searched Gilead's face. "You would likely fail."

Gilead wondered if the other man were trying to goad him. Arran had no apparent interest in the fate of the sleepers. "What do you care? You just want what your beloved king wants."

Arran's jaw clenched, and the green eyes sparked. "I have my own interests."

Gilead watched him carefully. He was trying hard not to be hasty. He used to call it decisiveness—but he had too many pieces he needed to line up to rush. He had no reason to trust either of these men. For all he knew, Joshua had sent them to entrap him. Joshua's easy camaraderie might be nothing more than the king's champion sensibly keeping his rival closer.

"I don't know which is the lie," he pointed out. "Robert has a family, and is under threat, and the two of you are being used to trap me. Or, Robert doesn't have a family, and couldn't even tell me he tried and failed. Or, worse, never tried."

"Who are you to judge him?" Arran demanded harshly, his voice filled with the angry judgment only a very young man could convey. "He is a good man and a good teacher. Unlike you, he is no soldier able to storm a castle, and he has taken care of the sleepers very well." A flock of birds broke skywards from the forest, and Arran looked warily into the trees.

"Not if they are starting to die," Gilead said. He kept his voice low.

"They've been in there too long," Arran cried.

Gilead grabbed his arm. "Shut it," he said.

Arran pulled free. He was stronger than he looked. "Think of your friends. Think of all the knowledge that will be lost if more of them die."

"And there we have it," Gilead said. This motivation he could almost believe. The kid wanted the lost magic of Earth. He had attached himself to McCrary and studied with him. He had been surprised to find that a soldier could read.

Arran looked away, obviously aware of the effect of

his words and that they said more about his intellectual curiosity than his humanity. "I am no hero," Arran said stiffly. "In fact, I am no warrior. But I can help waken your comrades."

Gilead spread his hands. He almost trusted Arran more than McCrary, but he was not going to rush into anything. "Let's talk after the tournament tomorrow. I'll be honest. I don't know that I trust either of you, and I don't know how to make this work."

"You could pretend to be sick," Arran said. "Robert could say he had to take you back to the keep."

Gilead laughed. "Do I look sick?"

Arran's eyes narrowed. "We could poison you. It might be safer than the tournament."

The day of the tournament dawned fair. The only clouds in the sky were small and puffy and moved rapidly in the winds aloft. The clouds even higher resembled shredded pennants of white scattered across the startling blue that arched so high above the large field. A field of green and blue stretched below the palace and close to the river, in an area that saw its share of flooding in late summer. Sheep had trimmed the grasses and blue wildflowers to a close crop, and tents and tables full of food, drink, art wares, and housewares crowded each other. Chickens roamed everywhere.

Gilead stopped at one table piled high with something that had the misfortune to smell like durian—but still got bought—and leaves stuffed with berries. Hardboiled eggs were selling for five pennies apiece, because of the convenience factor of not having to bring your own, and clove studded oranges rolled around the table. Gilead bought one of those and started peeling it. He couldn't believe it. He hadn't had an orange in five years subjective, and he felt the saliva gathering in his mouth. There had to be greenhouses, and he praised the settler who had brought an orange and cultivated the trees on Nwwwlf.

He saw Joshua walking toward him with a big, dumb grin on his face. "What are you doing?" Joshua asked. "We don't eat those things. They're for perfume."

"Oh, dear God," Gilead said with his mouth full, "that is why I was awakened—to eat your oranges and teach you all to do the same. My work here is done. May I leave now?"

"Are those from Earth?" Joshua asked, curious.

Gilead spat out a clove. "You bet they are, and, no, you can't have any."

The big, redheaded man laughed. "But how will I learn?"

Gilead removed more peel. He hadn't exactly waited until the whole thing was ready to shove as much as he could in his mouth. It wasn't the finest specimen of an orange he had ever seen, but it was certainly the most delicious. He popped a section and handed it to Joshua, who sniffed it as if he were testing a fine wine.

Then he ruined the effect by asking, "Is it like eating soap?"

"No," Gilead said, and made as if to snatch it back. "Earth cuisine is wasted on you. Except for the eggs, of course."

Joshua placed the segment of orange in his mouth and looked briefly alarmed. "Witchcraft," he muttered, and then paid the ludicrous price for an egg, but tossed it back to the vendor and asked her to peel it for him. "Certainly, sir," said the middle-aged woman. She was handsome, and had long eyelashes. She grinned at Joshua, and happily gave the egg a crack on the table. She finished her task in a matter of seconds, Joshua bowed, and she dimpled at her encounter with celebrity.

"They'll all know you, too, after tomorrow," Joshua declared loftily. They walked along a row of tables, and some of the owners tried to press free food onto Joshua.

Once they had left the tables behind, Joshua grew serious. "Listen, Gilead. I like you. It would all be very legendary if a magical sleeper were to best me tomorrow in front of the king and the whole country and all, but I want you to know I have no intention of letting you win."

Gilead gave Joshua the sober response he deserved. "Nor I you." He was lying. He knew he couldn't throw the minor matches, but he had no desire to be bound to the king as his personal champion. He had other plans. There were rumors of wilderness in the northeastern segment of the valley. It could be a good place to hide newly awakened sleepers, while still within the influence of Earth's bacteria and other offspring.

It wouldn't do, however, to mock or be cynical about the endeavor. "And," Gilead said, "we still have to get through today."

Joshua snorted. "Today will not be a problem. Today the trick is not to hurt our opponents. They'll just be boys straight in from the farm; couldn't hurt a bird. Tomorrow we'll see the better ones."

Joshua was right. Joshua's first fight was a wrestling match with a young man no bigger round than Joshua's thigh. They didn't bother with weight classes, Gilead observed. It would have been a kindness to the youngster had he been matched with someone of his own girth, but that might have left a tall weedy fellow to be blown over in a puff of wind in the last round, which would have held minimal entertainment value.

The rules required the contestants to work their way up a ladder. Last year's winner didn't get to rest until a worthy opponent appeared. He had to earn his spot all over again. On the other hand, they didn't want last year's winner defeated too early, so they allowed him to warm up with a few novices.

Gilead was surprised to learn that he was a long-odds favorite. The rumors of a soldier's powers had gained some traction. Now if he didn't win, he would be letting down some bettor. Weirdly, that bothered him. But, the more he thought about it, the more sense it made to avoid the honor. Ignoring his deeply competitive side, if he became the king's champion he would be tied to the king. Wherever the king had gone in the past year, Joshua had danced attendance. If Gilead didn't have another agenda it could be worthwhile, but he was not going to follow in Robert McCrary's path of surrender.

"It hardly counts, does it?" Gilead asked as Joshua came away from beating on the kid. "Kind of makes you wonder if you've still got it, doesn't it?"

Joshua scowled at him, suspicious of what Gilead was up to. "Got what?"

"Your skills," Gilead replied instantly.

"Don't you start that with me. I can see what you're trying to do."

A runner approached them, a very young man clad in orange and blue silks. There were several of them on the grounds, carrying messages and very conscious of the eyes that followed them. They had been chosen for looks and speed from amongst the families of the nobility. None were older than fifteen.

"My lords," he gasped. "I am sent by the king. Your presence is requested with all the other contestants in half an hour at the king's seat. He has an important announcement to make."

Gilead and Joshua eyed each other. "We accept the king's kind invitation," Joshua said, "and, please, do advise him that we are hurrying to attend him." Gilead merely spread his hands in front of him, as if nothing he said could match the fawning message already provided.

"Hurrying to his side," Gilead muttered. "Hurrying to him on bended knee, hurrying on our knees if only we could get up and walk like men. Hurrying—"

Joshua interrupted the gathering speed of Gilead's muttering. "You, too, will learn to love our king."

They passed another roped off arena, where Hank and his yellow hair wrestled some hapless soul, who would at least be able to state that he had lost to a worthy foe. Hank might not bother to claim the victory, but his opponent wouldn't know that.

The king sat on a raised dais where he held court amidst his loving subjects. He ignored the gathering knights, who cheerfully waited further word from their lord and master. The air was fine, no blood had been shed, only two bones broken, and the sky was shellacked a deep and vivid blue. Gilead felt like he was at a ball game, and wished heartily for someone to start wandering by with bottles of ice-cold beer. No one did, but he remained hopeful.

The king sat with his back to the river so that he could survey the activity in the fields. The river was wide at this part, not the Mississippi or anything, but wide enough you couldn't throw a stone across it. The water flowed placidly, with only the occasional log from upstream marring its glassy surface. A bird swept down on something only it could see, its piercing cry inducing paralysis in its prey, for it rose triumphantly from its dive, with something small and legged dangling from its beak.

When all the knights had gathered, the king rose and raised his arms for quiet. The sun reflected off his golden head, and the wide river curved away at his back like a bolt of fabric tossed out just for him. In all the high valley, he was a man of great power, and nature itself snuggled up to him.

The crowd immediately provided him the quiet he sought. He started with pleasantries and jokes, but when the crowd was laughing and happy he grew serious. "I have been thinking much about this tourney. It brings everyone together, gives the country boys a chance to try their skills against the knights, and—this year—one is even covered in glory as well as mud." He gestured to a lanky young man who grinned out from behind a thatch of straw-colored hair. A certain knight hung his head in shame. "Don't worry, Ell," the king called out, "there's always someone. We'll not throw you out of the palace. Yet."

He waited a moment before continuing. "But this year I have decided to add to the reward of winning the tournament. You all know that the winner of tomorrow's final match becomes my champion for the coming year. You all know how much I value that person." Everyone knew. Everyone knew how everyone else valued the champion and all his family, and what an opportunity it provided for being offered gifts, not just from the king, but from those who wanted access to him.

"To show that," the king said, "I will offer a boon to the winner. I have many things of value, much treasure—the greatest of which is the love of my people—and I want next year's champion to know that he may ask, that I want him to ask, for a boon, for his deepest heart's desire, and I will do everything in my power to grant it."

The crowds cheered, the knights cheered, and Gilead's heart leaped in his chest for the first time in a long while. Here was his chance, and he wouldn't have to storm the castle. The king would open its doors for him. He looked over at Joshua, and hunter's vision closed around the man, leaving nothing else in Gilead's sights. His grin was feral.

The next day was hotter, and the sun still blazed like a ball of brass in the blue sky when Gilead walked out to face Joshua. It had been inevitable, that they would face each other, but Gilead felt no qualms and he knew the other man had no thought of hesitation either. The fight was to first blood or a knockout. If one were lucky, the only blood spilled would be the small amount of pig blood held in a bladder fixed over their hearts. They both wore light, fitted, leather body armor.

When the bell rang at two minutes, if they were still in the ring they were to discard their swords. Then the fight went empty handed. Gilead had the greater reach, but Joshua more mass.

He had no intention of killing the man. The fight was not to the death, but sometimes a quick kill was easier and more economical than disabling someone. But he liked Joshua and meant to look out for him. Besides, killing the king's favorite might undermine what he wanted to ask for from the king.

The arena they stood in was a raised platform built especially so the spectators could see. There was a six foot drop should one of the combatants slip, and any fall would hit the crowd pressing up below. The standoff distances of civilization were missing here.

The king and his court did not suffer the disadvantages of the crowd. The king sat atop another, taller, raised structure in comfort and with a perfect view, the queen—Andrea's double—at his side. Their eyes met, and he looked quickly away. She filled him with nothing but yearning, and it was the wrong kind for the nature of the relationship they might actually have. The romances his soldier wife had avidly consumed were always full of such relativistic perils. He had thought them revolting. He had certainly never thought any would apply to him, and they didn't now.

She was waving at him. When he looked toward her, she blew him a kiss.

The king's face was stony, a cold mask beneath the blazing gold of his hair, and Gilead knew with utter certainty that the incentive Clarence had offered had not been meant for him. Etienne, the large blond who had taught Gilead to ride at Stampo, and who was no doubt well pleased with his new position and himself, stood at attention at the king's side. It was a singular honor for one so newly reinstated at the court.

There was no referee, and Clarence the only judge. Gilead had every intention of claiming that prize or shaming Clarence before all his people.

A courtier dressed in the highest style, fabric flowing off him everywhere, approached the king with great ceremony and knelt. He held out a small, green, velvet cushion atop which sat a wand of silver. The king took it gently in one hand, rose to his feet, and held the wand over his head, before arching high and slamming it into a bell hanging from the beams overhead.

The bell sounded with a joyful peal, and rang, echoing, across the arena, over the green sporting fields, into the woods, and back again.

Gilead knew with a dull finality that the speed of sound would be the highest speed he would ever experience again in his life—but he wouldn't be riding it.

As instructed, Gilead and Joshua raised their swords in salute to the king, and then to each other. The kiss of his steel against his own forehead felt cool and foolish, all at the same time, but it spoke to him, and he appreciated the vivid reminder of what was to come. Today was not a good day to die, but it could happen—to either of them. There were no safeguards on the blades.

In the moment before the match began, he was reminded of how he felt before the drops he had done in powered armor as a nineteen-year old, and this was not very different. He felt the same cool chill along his neck, the same hollow sensation in his stomach, and the same contradictory fire in his heart.

His lips spread in a smile, because now, when no other choices remained to him, he did know how to fight. He lunged and parried almost in the same moment, for Joshua, too, chose a thrust to the bladder.

It was clear they both held high opinions of their own speed.

The joint maneuver having failed, they circled.

Gilead had trained with Joshua, and knew at least some of his tells, the flick of the eye, the indrawn breath. Joshua's boots hid the lift of the toes that Gilead had noticed in wrestling matches, and he let his vision go wide to absorb all the inputs.

Joshua's low-line cut made Gilead parry, but Joshua's move had been a feint, and Gilead had to parry, parry again, and again as he found himself backing across the shining, wooden floor. Gilead was not alone in his desire to win this match and whatever request the king might grant.

"Look over there," Joshua muttered, his own face wreathed in a grin as big as the river. The small humor signaled overconfidence, and Gilead dropped low, his sword aloft as his only shield, as he swept Joshua's leg with his foot. He had not shared his use of such tactics in his practice in the palace, but Joshua rebalanced, lifted the threatened foot, and brought his sword down in a flashing arc at Gilead's leg. Gilead withdrew faster than Joshua could strike, but felt the glancing pressure against the light leather of his boot, and resolved to be quicker next time, just to have the margin.

The crowd cheered, liking the show, and, large birds

circled overhead as if waiting to feast on the outcome. Drawn perhaps by the noise of steel on steel, which presaged dining when heard amongst crowds, they didn't know this was not a field for a real battle.

The men were too evenly matched, and even when Gilead drove hard in an attempt to take advantage of his highly oxygenated blood, Joshua showed no sign of weakening.

The bell rang, after what seemed like hardly any time. Even at the equivalent of an all-out sprint, both were breathing well enough. Gilead wondered if his time in cold sleep had lost him his edge. Fighting Joshua was too much like fighting one of Gilead's own comrades in arms.

Two men took the swords. Now the rivals would fight empty handed.

This ring lacked the accompaniments Gilead was used to from his own time. No one offered him water, a rest, or a quick rub down.

The king signaled, and the attendants began working on the buckles to his cuirass, which had been recently cleaned and oiled and came off easily. Gilead suffered the public undressing impassively.

The king made another signal.

Joshua grinned at him from across the ring, and lifted his shirt over his head. "Your boots," said Gilead's attendant. Gilead sighed, stripped his shirt, and allowed the man to remove his boots. The finely polished wood of the dais didn't look like it would produce splinters, and his feet had regained all their callouses. The wind curled around his wet ribcage, and he took the shirt back and used it to dry himself.

The blue sky, high and distant, held a pair of circling birds. Their wings, refined by a separate evolutionary line, appeared invisible at different angles, and their screams pierced the distance before fading in the air above the throng of people.

King and crowd surveyed the two men.

The redheaded man stood like a giant bull, stepped from a painting of the flames of hell, his fiery hair blending into the tanned face and neck. The dark fire was a counterpoint to the pale skin of his shoulders and torso, which glowed white, almost alabaster in the sun. He was powerfully muscled, and, clearly, always, ate his eggs for breakfast.

The other they considered an ancestor, despite his having contributed nothing to their genetic heritage. Still, he was a starman. He had lost the pallor of the sleeping quarters, but the dark brown hair and pale brown eyes, the long muscles that fired so quickly and stood out in stark relief now like some sort of anatomy lesson, showed how quickly he had recovered from his centuries of enforced sleep.

Gilead felt no fear regarding Joshua. He merely feared bad luck, a moment of inattention. He took a breath and shifted into hard focus. Another stutter breath brought him the rest of his force. Some in the crowd might have thought he prayed.

The attendants brought their charges to the center of the ring, keeping them a body length apart at the outset. Joshua left his hands, flexed and loose, arrogantly low. Gilead had no intention of closing. It would devolve into a wrestling match, he had no doubt, but first he meant to batter. In this phase, the head was fair game.

He took two shots to Joshua's head with his fists, but the blade of his foot connected with his real target, the front of Joshua's thighbone, in a downward stomp. Joshua showed no sign of having felt it. They separated, and when next they came within reach of each other, Joshua threw a right which Gilead dodged and blocked while grabbing the arm, pivoting inside Joshua's guard and smashing the forearm of an elbow strike across Joshua's neck. Joshua didn't cooperate, and the strike choked him up, but only a little. Still, on his way out of Joshua's hold Gilead left another blow up Joshua's thigh, this time with his shin. So very intimate as they were, Gilead saw that one register. If one didn't condition the legs, it was like being hit in the bone with an iron bar, as Gilead remembered well from his own youth.

The warriors of Nwwwlf spent little time with the *make wara*, Gilead knew.

By the fourth blow to the same leg, Joshua's sunny joy in battle had morphed into a very different emotion. The crowd was not impressed with Gilead's battering of their champion's legs, it being a different approach to wearing out an opponent, which meant it had to be cheating. The noise of them explaining this to each other was loud and ugly, and each time Gilead landed another crippling blow, they filled the air with, first, moaning, and then booing.

Joshua had had enough, and lunged for Gilead's legs, the implements of his own torture, in an attempt to get the other man on the ground. Gilead let him come in, but, guiding the back of his head, shoved his knee into the other man's golden face. This did not constitute cheating and brought some cheers.

Gilead threw Joshua back, and the other man staggered, still unsteady from the knee in his face.

He blinked and shook his head while Gilead walked in and methodically and scientifically hit him first on one side of the jaw, then the other, and knocked him out.

The crowd roared, dissatisfied no more.

Hands on hips, the wind bringing an instant cooling sensation to his overheated and finally still body,

Gilead stood over Joshua's unconscious form. One attendant began the slowest count to ten he had ever heard, and the wind had time to lift his hair and bathe his face while the sun tried to return the heat the wind robbed him of.

By the count of seven, the crowd, ever fickle, was counting, too—loudly, rhythmically, and with great gusto in celebration of the fall of their champion. Finally, "ten!" shouted the attendant and the crowd together.

Now Gilead, his face serenely triumphant, but pale eyes watchful, turned from Joshua to the king.

Clarence was good at speaking to crowds. He rose to his feet and, when he raised both arms, brought them all to quiet.

"We have a new champion," he called, and waited. Loud cheering erupted, and the attendants lifted both of Gilead's arms in a half-dressed mirror of the king's pose. He felt as if he'd been dropped in the stone age, but with a lot more carpentry. He swallowed, and tried not to think whether the other sleepers would thank him for wakening them to this. They might be happier if they woke in a different century, one more civilized and less like a giant fraternity party.

Or, they might not wake at all.

He waited. He would not second-guess his plan. It was a good one. The king had made an offer and he planned to take it. It was perfect—the king would change the law, but only to honor his word, which should make it all okay in the eyes of the people. And, Gilead planned to offer reasons that would appeal to the leader so bent on war with the Pan.

The king, too, looked as if he had been thinking, for he closed off the cheering only a moment before it started to die out of its own accord. He stood, now, and one hand gripped the rail in front of him. "This man is a stranger to us, but he is a sleeper from the starship, one of those who chose to leave Earth for a new world. It wasn't this world, and he slept through the ship losing its way and reaching Nwwwlf, but he is awake now. No matter how different from us—and no matter how strange his ways of combat—he is our new champion."

The cheering was now lukewarm at best, an attempt to be polite. Had Joshua won, the speech and the response would have been different, Gilead knew.

"Gilead Tan," the king went on, and his voice carried far enough that everyone in the crowd could hear. "As the new champion, you are due a boon. I know that you have likely not given it much thought, since I only announced it yesterday. I am happy to let you think carefully, and we may discuss it tomorrow."

Gilead knew with certainty that Clarence would not have delayed Joshua's request. Joshua would have asked for something reasonable, after all. Who knew what Gilead might want?

"Sire," said Gilead, and he, too, pitched his voice to carry far. "You are too generous, and there is no need for me to wait. I already know my wish." *It's why I made sure to win,* he thought. *If I'd thrown the fight to get away from you, no one would ever have known.*

Clarence raised the hand that wasn't gripping the rail. "No need, Gilead. No need. I want to make sure you have carefully thought through your heart's desire."

"I know my heart's desire," Gilead said, and his voice rang loud and clear across the crowd and the field. The crowd fell silent, and the birds called out.

Clarence's face was stone.

Gilead plowed on. "I wish nothing more than that you grant permission for my comrades to be awakened. One of them died, before I was awakened—they have been sleeping too long."

"Gilead," the king's voice was gentle, "I do not wish

you to waste your wish. It is the law of this land that only one sleeper may be awakened every fifty years. Still, I will let you sleep on your request." The crowd murmured approvingly.

It was his only chance. He felt it slipping away, and he couldn't tell why. He must persuade Clarence, and the crowd of people, too. "Then waive the law, make an exception. You could have almost two hundred people, many with my strength, to protect this land and defeat the Pan." A few cheers greeted this, but they were isolated and stopped quickly.

It was not evident that this was the right thing to have said, as the men in the crowd, the king, and his knights, all pondered the thought of two hundred more men with Gilead Tan's quickness, strength, and agility, and, perhaps, his same disregard for their traditions.

It didn't go over well.

Still the king kept his voice gentle, but with his face a frozen mask, the blue eyes intense, it was clear that his voice used up all his control. "I think that is enough, Gilead. Enjoy your victory."

"Sire," Gilead said. The air cooled the sweat on his body to salt, and the chill grew inside as well as outside. His hands were clenched at his side, and he wished he did not sound like a pleading child.

He grew angry. "You gave your word," he said. "You gave your word, and I mean you to keep it."

"Gilead Tan," Clarence said with righteous wrath, "You must respect our history. You must respect our traditions. Your ways are not ours."

"And my people are not yours," Gilead roared. It was too much. He could not put up with this man and his righteous idiocy.

The king's head jerked back, but still he showed no change in his face. "I will not awaken your wife."

"I don't have a wife anymore," Gilead said. His voice

still carried, as if pitched for a battle in this land, where there'd be no comm unit at your throat. The crowd was deathly silent, enthralled. "You have my wife. The queen is clearly her great, great granddaughter." He gestured to the queen, who looked puzzled, then pale, then red as the scarf at her neck.

"Do not speak of my queen," the king said. He was visibly furious now. "You have forfeited my championship. You have forfeited your right to ask a gift. You are uncouth and loathsome. You wish to join your companions? So be it."

He gestured to the captain of the guard. That man called on several others, and Etienne joined the contingent exiting the king's box. Joshua had disappeared from the ring, whether regaining consciousness or carried off during Gilead's exchange with Clarence, Gilead didn't know.

Gilead watched as the booted and armored men approached through the crowd. He was acutely conscious of his own lack of cover. Gilead wore nothing but his breeches, as the chill fingers of the wind persisted in reminding him. Etienne wore a large grin on his big face.

Gilead was strong, and Gilead was quick, and Gilead had fought more than one person at a time more than once in his life. Nor did he suffer any qualms about hurting these men.

They made sure to surround him as they started to climb into the ring, but he landed a flying front kick on the chin of the nearest man crawling over the brightly festooned railing, and sent that one opponent back into the crowd. Two others replaced him from the side.

Gilead vaulted over them and landed on the railing like a gymnast. A quick look into the crowd showed him what a bad idea joining them would be. Fortunately, he balanced perpendicular to the king's box, which allowed him room to run. There were horses behind that box, if he could reach one of the beasts.

He aimed to clear the crowd, which was small between the ring and the king's box, but a long wooden staff stopped his sprint, and knocked him back into the arena. Etienne was there to catch him, and Gilead, held around the waist with his feet in the air, put all the compressed power of his body behind his punch to the other man's jaw.

Etienne dropped Gilead, but three others fell on him, and four others held his limbs down. Etienne looked woozy, but he managed a kick to Gilead's head.

Gilead felt the kick to his ribs by a booted foot, heard the internal crack, and was hauled to his feet. They turned him to face Clarence, so the king could see better. The king took in the scene with grim pleasure.

Gilead had nothing to lose. "Free them," Gilead demanded. He felt a sucker punch to a kidney, and then far too many of the blows that followed, certain he faced his own death.

Arran was not a soldier. He did not fight. He often scorned those who did. He had not meant to come to Gilead's match against Joshua, but it was easy. Everyone made way for the young lordling who danced attendance on the new sleeper. Watching the match between Gilead and Joshua had neither exhilarated nor soothed Arran. Gilead's plea for the sleepers filled him with much stronger emotion that the merely physical fear he had felt for both men in the foolish sword fight, a match that could have deprived them all of two good men.

But Gilead's plea for the sleepers was not well reasoned, and Arran listened, first in rage, and then in horror, to the king's response to the sleeper's request. At the first crack in Gilead's ribs, Arran finally moved.

Later, he would say he didn't know how he found himself on the platform, what he intended, or why this sleeper had to be kept alive when there were others, but as he reached for the pole in one corner and prayed he wasn't too late, at least one pair of hands shoved him up and none pulled him back. It would have been good if whoever had helped him had also joined him on the platform in defense of the fallen Gilead, but he paid no attention.

There was so much noise.

So many of the men were taller than Arran, and all were wider and denser than the twenty-year old. There were maybe half a dozen in a circle around Gilead, and the rest held his limbs—for no necessary reason at that point.

Arran spared a glance for the king, whose lips were pulled back to show white teeth. "Cousin!" Arran called out—it was one last chance for Clarence to redeem himself—but Arran expected no response and received none.

From his side where he always kept them, Arran pulled the batons free by their handles. It did not enter his head until later, the futility of one scholarly young man standing against the thugs who battered Gilead. At the time it was enough to deaden an elbow, to shatter a knee on the backswing, to strike a man in the head when he turned too sharply. Arran had a battle cry of his own it turned out, and it mingled with Gilead's hoarse imprecations—that were really just screams—to free the sleepers.

CHAPTER 8

THE BED ROLLED, CREAKED, AND bumped Gilead, every move a reminder that he had been beaten broken and bloody. He lay flat on his back, and he hurt. He tried to put a hand to his ribs, but found he was shackled at wrist and ankle. His head, at least, was on something soft, and a probing tongue found all his teeth intact, but his mouth swollen. Someone had punched him to shut him up. He had been unable to help screaming at the end of it all, but had forced the cries into two simple words, "Free them." This tactic had proved no more persuasive than his attempt to take Clarence up on his phony offer.

Breathing in too deeply hurt both his bones and his lungs, but the movement told him someone had bandaged his ribs. He supposed he should be grateful, but the sun beat into his eyes, and the sweat running off him fell into flesh that was still raw.

"Hey," he tried to say, but it came out as a moan. That was embarrassing. He was glad Joshua hadn't participated in the beating.

With his eyes shut against the sun, he heard sounds. Birds mewed above, horses hooves clopped along a dirt road, and the rhythmic creak of tack and jingle of harness told him he was in a cart.

He pondered the wisdom of keeping quiet, of letting his captors believe him still unconscious, but tried, "Hey," again. This time his voice was a little louder.

His throat was raw, and he was embarrassed all over again.

He decided that being chained spread-eagled in the back of a cart after a beating was sufficiently embarrassing all by itself that he didn't need to sweat the rest of it. He swallowed against the dryness.

"Hey," he called again.

He heard new hooves, more deliberate than the steady walking of the others, as if someone had brought his mount to a trot.

"Gilead?" said the doctor's voice.

"Robert," Gilead said. He found that effort enough.

"You aren't a people person, are you, son?" the doctor said.

He didn't need that. He hadn't known the doctor had a sadistic streak, but it made sense. Doctors liked being around people in pain, or people who were sick and weak and vulnerable. It wasn't attractive. Gilead decided he'd share his new insight with Robert the next time he was up for a good chat.

"Get me out of here, Robert."

"Sure. Don't go anywhere."

He would have preferred to lose consciousness again, but he wasn't so lucky.

Voices sounded up ahead, and there was some shouting, but it sounded like directions more than an argument, and the cart stopped. The sky looked exactly the same as it had before, blue, blue and more blue. Maybe there was a hint of lime green in it.

Then the cart turned sharply and made its way, bumping, off the road. It was agony, and he worked hard not to cry out. The shade the jarring path took him to was small comfort after the ride, but he accepted that much gratefully. The shade held more than a hint of lime, and Gilead would have given one of his ribs for a piece of creamy, cooling, Key Lime pie.

"For Chrissakes, let him out. He couldn't hurt your

little finger if he wanted to." It was the doctor being rude again.

Someone let the end of the cart down. He closed his eyes and looked as weak as he could. It didn't take a lot of effort.

He must have done a good job, for he felt the clasps on his ankles being undone. He lay still.

"I got the rope," a voice said, and Gilead abandoned what were admittedly stupid plans to try to make a run for it. Then he changed his mind. Maybe the rope wasn't to catch him. Maybe they'd brought him out here to hang him.

He swore, and heard McCrary laugh. The last manacle came off his wrist, and he sat up.

The doctor appeared at the side of the cart. "They're not going to hang you. The king wants you put back to sleep."

That was ominous enough. Gilead blinked in reply.

"No, really, he wants you put back in your sleeping cell."

"I need to get up," Gilead said.

McCrary sent around one of the men in his escort to help him rise, and he cautiously moved himself to the end of the cart, where someone had obligingly let the end down. It was a low cart, and his feet reached the ground when he swung them over the edge.

Standing wasn't easy.

Arran came around the side of the cart, took one look at him, and carefully pulled Gilead's arm across his shoulder. He held him around the waist as they walked over to a seating area with a rug and three folding chairs.

Etienne stood at a distance, watching them and frowning.

"What's he doing here?" Gilead asked as he sat down.

"Etienne's being sent back to Stampo," Arran said,

letting go of Gilead and stepping away. "He's not happy about it, but they figured they needed someone big to keep an eye on you. He blames you." Everyone had a sadistic streak when a man was down.

One of the guardsmen passed around food, and Gilead started peeling his boiled egg. His hands shook.

"Here," Arran said gruffly and took the egg from him. Arran handed Gilead a flask. "Drink."

His thirst could never be slaked, but finally Gilead took the flask from his lips. The tepid water tasted better than any he'd ever had in his life, and he'd kept a bit in his mouth to cherish it, before swallowing. "Your hospital sucks, Robert."

The doctor tossed his eggshells behind him into the bush. "It's not my system. Chaining you seems to have been overkill."

Arran was frowning at Gilead. The green eyes held a note of real anger. "Dr. McCrary did his best. He kept them from killing you."

McCrary snorted. "It wasn't me. I just got the king to agree that you should live. Arran was the one who went out there and made sure of it. Did you know he uses those to club people?" He pointed to the two, heavy, short sticks Arran wore at his belt. Gilead was surprised to find he had no trouble picturing the young man wielding them like police batons. That he did so against the mob that had been methodically kicking Gilead to death gave him pause. Again, Gilead was reminded of a certain young lieutenant he hadn't really liked, but this time his recollections were warmer.

"The king's guard helped," Arran said drily.

"Never mind how reluctant they were to do it." McCrary was equally dry.

Gilead looked at Arran carefully. He was unmarked. The crowd had not turned on one of the king's courtiers. "Does the king hate you, too, now?"

"Not at all," Arran said. "I saved him from letting a sleeper be killed."

Gilead nodded. "Clever."

"Unlike you," Robert said. "What were you thinking, son?"

Gilead stared at the doctor blankly. "What do you mean?"

"Leave him alone, Robert." Arran's voice was harsh.

"You should have trusted us, Gilead," Robert said around a mouthful of sandwich. "We'd have told you not to do something so stupid." Robert's bedside manner matched his hospital system.

"Asking for my 'boon'? That was stupid?"

"It was," Arran agreed reluctantly. "The offer of riches wasn't meant for you. The king is not your friend. He was so excited about you before he got you, but you were so very much not who he had been looking for."

"That's why I won the match," Gilead exclaimed, astonished at the course the conversation was taking, and not just because he wouldn't have minded a little more TLC and a lot less scolding. "So I could ask."

The doctor shook his head. He held off on taking another bite before talking this time, but stared with deep longing at his sandwich. "I understand you were grieving, son, but you weren't thinking. You spent all your time exhausting yourself in training, and you didn't do any politicking. If the crowd had agreed with you, you might have forced the king's hand."

Providing an objective, and purely helpful critique, Arran said, "And then you said a number of foolish things. Did you really think he wanted to be surrounded by more people like you? Angry and stronger than his men?"

"Again," McCrary said. "What were you thinking?"

"They wouldn't have been angry at him if he'd woken them all up." Gilead would have swatted at a frog that jumped on his leg, but it required too much effort. "He'd've been their savior."

McCrary batted the frog away. Both men stared at Gilead, and neither said anything about what he'd said to the king about the queen. But it didn't need saying, and even the doctor had some mercy in his soul.

The part of Gilead that didn't hurt—which was an admittedly small part—wasn't too upset. He had not meant to return to Stampo in his current condition, and he would have to get better fast. His plans needed some modification, but he'd soon be where he needed to be. And no one would suspect him of a deliberate ploy. He would have laughed, if he hadn't known it would hurt.

"You're lucky you're alive," Robert said, and went back to his sandwich.

Arran had finished his own sandwich, and brushed crumbs from his breeches. He wore no jacket, and his shirt was open at the neck. If Gilead hadn't been so miserable and burning so badly even in the shade, it would have been a fine picnic.

"The king wanted you put back in cold sleep immediately," Arran said. "The doctor told him—in front of many people—that you would die if you went back under in your current condition."

"Am I being traded in?" Gilead asked. "For a better sleeper?"

"You are," McCrary said. "We tried to let you recuperate at the king's palace until you were well enough to travel on your own, but he wanted you gone. You're to be kept guarded and chained until you're well enough for a cold sleep."

"Who decides that?" Gilead asked.

"I do," Arran said. "I am conducting the king's business when it comes to you."

Gilead snorted. "I guess I better be nice to you."

A rare flash of amusement lit the other's face. Arran almost smiled. "I guess you had better," he said.

Gilead held out the last half of his sandwich to Arran. "I can't finish this." One didn't waste food on Nwwwlf. There was enough, but no one threw it out. Ever. "You take it."

Arran waved it away, now visibly amused. "You don't have to be that nice."

"I'm not," Gilead admitted. "I really can't eat it."

"Well, then." Arran rose briskly to his feet. "Put him back in the cart," he called to the guards.

"Hey," Gilead said. "Don't have them chain me."

Arran ignored him, waiting for the guards. "Be careful with him," he told them. "We want him healthy enough to put back in the sleeping cell."

"Are we chaining him, then, sir?" one asked.

"One foot will suffice," Arran said. "He can't even finish his food. I doubt he'll be gnawing through his own leg."

It took longer to return to the fort in the mountain than it had taken to leave it. They travelled slowly as the land rose, with frequent stops over the course of several days, and the guardsmen took to watching for wild chickens. They kept them as pets and for their eggs. Gilead did not even have a chicken he could call his own.

They came over a rise at the end of a long day, Gilead still in the cart. The winding road curved up through switchbacks, looked over gentled slopes and sheer drops, and finally led them to the walled entrance. As mountain roads went, it was a good one. It might have been blasted and cut centuries back, but it was maintained, and the cart was no worse on it than on the dirt road in the valley.

Stampo was much as Gilead remembered it. Having spent time in the palace in the valley, where the stones houses were small and the wooden ones not much bigger, and only the palace itself showed signs of the construction capabilities of Gilead's time, he recognized the mountain fortress as being of a different age and larger scale. He wondered what had led the original settlers to build this structure at so inconvenient a location. Maybe they had been concerned about the river flooding. In any event, they placed their sleeping comrades, with neither their knowledge nor consent, in a mountain fastness built by whatever machines they had brought. He looked forward to the electricity in the labs.

The thought gave him pause. He had recovered enough to start contemplating escape. He would have to. It would be a black eye for Arran, and McCrary might be put at risk, but likely not. He would have to do it without their assistance.

He would recover more quickly than anyone would expect. He was feeling much improved already, at least on the outside. His insides still felt bruised and raw, and every now and then he lost his voice completely. That was still embarrassing.

The details of his planning had to take into account his status as a heavily wounded captive. First, he planned to wake his four friends and as many other soldiers as still lived—in that order.

The civilians were another matter. They wouldn't get the surge of energy a combat wake would supply the former soldiers. They would need the more gentle resuscitation offered by a full flush, and for that he would need to take the keep. He knew the five of them could do it, and there would have to be volunteers from the others he planned to rescue. He would come back for the civilians, even though the Marss would plan for the attempt. Gilead hadn't been shy about what he wanted.

But where would they go? He could hide them all in the northwestern corner of the valley, but he didn't rule out finding the Pan. Maybe it was only their criminals who kidnapped children. That kidnapping happened didn't necessarily mean it was a foreign policy. Or, worst case, the Pan were lost in the stone age somewhere, and he would dream longingly of subsistence farming and the obligatory feudal overlord. Nonetheless, he needed to, first, get better, next, free as many as he could, third, get the hell out of the valley, and, finally, return for the rest. Details to follow.

Both ankles were chained to the cart again, as if Arran wanted to make sure Stampo knew he had the sleeper under control, and Gilead sat with his hands chained together. It was marginally more comfortable than having them fixed to the side of the cart, but the chain was short, too short to make a good noose.

The doctor oversaw Gilead's exit from the cart. The guards left his wrists chained, and he hobbled slowly into the keep.

"Are you okay?" Robert asked softly.

Gilead sagged. He was weak enough that it might have been real. He had no reason to let everyone know of any improvement, and wasn't playing at fortitude right now. "Been better," he said harshly. He still swore at Arran every time he saw him. The chains were ridiculous. They could have just put an arrow in him had he run for it.

He tried to focus on his plans. If he could only wake one of them, whom would he pick, Mason or Llew? Mason was more phlegmatic and would likely handle things better, but Llew would be more entertaining, point out the absurdity of it all, make him laugh.

He shook himself. His mind was wandering and he

needed to pay attention to his route and location. They took him back through the courtyard, and off to the east he saw the field where he'd ridden his first horse. The shadows, a strange mix of indigo on green, were long across it.

They reached the door to the building itself, and his heart was suddenly filled with despair. It was dark inside, with a single oil lamp burning in the large hall.

Andrea was lost to him, and he would rescue his friends to this barbarism.

He knew the despair arose out of his physical condition, but it hurt him, and all he wanted was to lie down.

Still, he tracked the route to his room. It was the last one they'd given him, and, chained to his bed, he listened to the key turn in the lock.

When he awoke it was dark, and the weakness was gone.

CHAPTER 9

I T WAS EASY FOR GILEAD to pretend extreme weakness
and lassitude during the day when he spent nights
raiding the keep's kitchen, workshops, stables,
and henhouses. He had his eyes on some chickens.
They—his optimistic "they"—wouldn't survive the
wilds without the birds.

Gilead had spent the first full day after his arrival
picking the lock on his chain. It was awkward but
doable. He had eyed the small wires behind the firewood
with some skepticism, but one of them doubled nicely
as a key for his manacles. It was a relief to remove
them, and very difficult to put them back on. He
wondered who had placed the wires and why. There
was nothing so blatant as a key, but another couple
of the wires fashioned together served as a key to the
bars on the window.

The first night out he simply left the keep with the
stolen flashlight he had taken into the catacombs that
housed the sleepers. The smaller moon was full, and,
coupled with the light of the larger red orb, he was
able to see well enough. Hours of searching led him to
a small clearing higher up the mountain, the portion
that had not been shorn to make room for Stampo long
ago. The glade had water from a spring, thick, scrubby
grass, and distance from the keep.

The second night he brought food, which he stored
in the high branches of a convenient tree to protect

against the ground-based inhabitants, whether furry or hooved, of the clearing on the mountain. The kitchen was not so much guarded as minded, and the kitchen boy assigned to tend the fire had fallen asleep in front of it, never noticing Gilead pillaging the hardtack, jerky, and pemmican.

Gilead had no idea how far he and his friends would go or what they would find, but there was a big world out there, and someone with guts had to have quit Clarence's kingdom in the past three centuries. Statistics required it, and the exploration genes should have been strong in these people. He planned to find some of them.

When Arran brought him news of the two deaths on their fifth day back, Mason's death broke him all over again. He had not known the other sleeper, but Mason, Mason had been his friend and comrade in arms. Mason had known Andrea. And, now, Mason was gone, too.

They offered to remove his leg irons and let him attend the funerals if he wished, and he did. The cemetery lay downhill of the keep, nestled in a hollow cleared of trees. He saw a ewe and a lamb. The sheep kept the blue-green grass manageable, if uneven. The old gravestones were mostly rough, the names worn off.

He had not known her name, and did not recognize the other dead sleeper, a woman with red hair and freckles. They showed him Mason's body, and the sight of the familiar face, with Mason's short, flattened nose, and jowls that would have drooped had he lived long enough, brought back the despair. In a single breath he wept at the barbaric grave like a babe.

He didn't go out that night, choosing the beer that Arran left him, and dreamt of Mason and Llew—who let no one call him Llewellyn—drowning in their sleeper cells, demanding that Gilead let them out, swearing at him for not moving fast enough, wasting time in healing and preparation when he should just get them the hell out.

He woke in the morning, sweating and trembling, and wondering if he had a fever. The doctor and Arran fussed over him, and a woman from the kitchen brought him broth. She fussed over him, too, and scolded the men for not giving Gilead an ice bath when he was burning up. She set about procuring one.

Etienne came by to say his farewells, very solemnly, as if they were long lost brothers, and he hadn't been one of the party that kicked Gilead almost to death. Gilead mumbled his thanks, but otherwise just sweated as Etienne congratulated Gilead on his victory over Joshua Calhoun, thanked Gilead for his time with them, joked about being more careful with the next sleeper himself, and offered his condolences on Gilead's lost comrades. Gilead found it immensely irritating, as if the man did it only to tell others he had said the final farewells to the ostracized sleeper. He would regale the kitchen with Gilead's condition, and it was a toss-up as to whether he would boast or sheepishly admit to the role he had played in Gilead's cracked ribs, bruised face, and fevered condition.

Finally, unable to bear it any longer, Gilead said, "I'm going back to the sleeping quarters for a while, Etienne, that's all."

Etienne gazed at him sorrowfully, as if he suspected worse than that for a man in Gilead's sweating condition. You could die of a fever, on Nwwwlf. "But I will not be here when you come back. Perhaps you will meet one of my grandchildren."

Gilead lay back on the bed, the chain he deigned to wear during the daytime laying across his stomach. "I need to sleep now, Etienne. Thank you for coming." Thank you for coming to my deathbed, he thought.

He hoped he didn't say it aloud. He wished someone would take the chain off. It really bothered him. Even with his nights without it and the bandages in which McCrary wrapped him, his wrists and ankles were raw. Everything bothered him as he sweated, even his teeth. He wondered if Arran had put something in the beer.

"Another one died," Dr. McCrary said. They had been back at Stampo eight days, and this was the third death in the sleeping quarters after Gilead's friend and the redheaded woman.

"I'll send word to the king," Arran told him, and his stomach tightened. The sleepers needed to stop dying. The redheaded woman had been an engineer, and that one's death bothered Arran mightily. So much had been lost with her mind.

"That's not going to do anyone any good, and you know it." Robert's voice was harsh, and he sounded his age. The first dead sleeper, the man they had attempted to wake right before Gilead, had bothered the doctor, and he had mentioned the man more than once while they were at the palace. Upon their return to the keep, Robert had insisted on checking them all, and the indicators had reported two very well preserved cadavers. Arran almost wished the doctor hadn't checked. It made putting Gilead back in his sleeping cell a task that filled him with no joy, a horrific prospect.

Arran had pinned certain hopes on Gilead, but Gilead didn't seem likely to come through. Gilead despaired and acted as if he faced a death sentence, and it might well be one, given the fates of so many others.

Dr. McCrary was talking. "There were two last year."

Arran was surprised. "When?"

"In the summer, when you were doing your courtier thing."

"You didn't tell me."

The physician shrugged. "I sent a message to the king, asking him to let me wake some, so I was checking them. I have friends in there, too. I dreaded facing them, but I didn't want them to die."

That explained why the king had taken Arran aside before they left this time, and cryptically said, "Don't forget. Robert is a sleeper, too. I rely on his lack of courage and his age, but keep an eye on him." It was not a conversation to share with its subject.

Later, at night, when Arran walked out onto the top of the wall, with its parapet for soldiers to defend the keep, he looked down into the valley. The city was too far to see, at a little over ten kilometers as the crow flew, in the dark. Dr. McCrary had once shown the court pictures of Earth from space, hundred of kilometers above the surface of the planet. The blaze of lights powered by electricity was a sight he would never forget.

Arran wanted that for Nwwwlf.

Maybe power plants had been impossible to pass along when the settlers first landed, what with the need to clear and build, and with the lack of equipment for a virgin world. The settlers had originally been heading for what Robert called a second wave planet, one that had already undergone some modicum of taming. Robert considered it a miracle that the reactor and the sleepers had been de-orbited and installed in their safe haven in the mountain. The isolated location selected for the sleepers had to signal a conflict amongst the original settlers. Likely, some had wanted all the sleepers awakened, and some had thought it best to make that impossible. Hence, the mountain.

He had mentioned all this to the doctor once,

and McCrary had said it was all ridiculous, and it wasn't worth it trying to second-guess a bunch of obvious idiots.

Now, pondering the darkened valley below, Arran thought that maybe it wasn't ridiculous. Tragic, yes, but that was because if the original settlers had had the support of a few more minds and a few more hands, perhaps they could have made whatever critical progress was necessary to give their descendants a better life, not the poverty of their current existence. They could have electricity and automobiles, medicine and space travel, and fewer deaths in childbirth. His mother might still be alive.

Arran shook his head. It did him no good to dwell on what hadn't happened. He had only to look at himself to see how it had come about. Those who didn't like the decision had not been strong enough, in character or numbers, to stop whoever thought that keeping the sleepers down was a good idea.

He was no different, despite his entry into the ring with Gilead. That had been mindless, as far as he could tell when he puzzled over it later, and so didn't count as any measure of real courage. He might be hoping that Gilead would do something, pull off some feat of daring, but Arran himself had methodically, aside from dropping a few wires in Gilead's room, followed all the king's orders, and, in not too long a time, would have Gilead put to sleep. All the while he would also wait for Gilead to take care of the injustice, Gilead to awaken the others, and Gilead to bring all that missing knowledge back to life.

He took a deep, shuddering breath. He had to do something. Ever since the sentencing of the farmers, he had been experiencing a growing unease that perhaps Clarence wasn't always right. He remembered for the thousandth time Clarence's feral smile at Gilead's beating.

Arran's long admiration for his older cousin, his natural love for his ruler, all made the thought of disagreement, much less disapproval, disquieting in the extreme. If Arran did anything to help Gilead avoid his fate, it would mean disobeying his king, his king who trusted him to do what others could not.

There were many warriors. There were few scientists. But there were many ways to be a scientist, and it was not kings who had won the stars for Earth.

Maybe Gilead needed just one more ally.

When the fever broke and the despair lifted, Gilead's resolve returned.

He had to save as many as he could in the first run. He had to. The chance of anyone else dying in the sleeping quarters would be on his conscience if he didn't take action.

He recognized the wild whipsawing of his emotions for part of his recovery period. The system that made his recovery so quick depleted other reserves he knew from basic training long ago. It was something he forgot every time.

He resolved to keep working toward his goals, even if the despair hit again. He would just ride it out.

Now, he called up in memory the list of names and the locations that Robert had let him see. He had not consciously taken them all in, but, with a little focus, he saw Llewellyn Engberg listed as 154B. He didn't dare the gentle wake for Llew that he had received. Trundling an entire sleeping cell into Robert's lab begged for failure. He would do a combat wake and hope for the best. Part of him callously considered practicing on someone he didn't know, but Llew would not have approved.

He had grown to recognize the quality of the quiet in the keep. The movement of humans led to the movement of other things in the walls. They weren't rats—humanity had finally, after a few disasters, figured out how not to bring rats to other planets— but they were small and indigenous and thrived on the leavings of humans. It reached that quiet now. He pulled himself off the bed and reached below the mattress for his improvised keys. He did not risk his work for comfort. Someone might come in at any point during the day.

Silently, so the guard would not hear, he undid the manacles.

He laid the chain back across his legs for camouflage. Next, he undid his hands. He had a journey tonight, down the wall, around the fort and into the catacombs. His hands free, he placed the chains to his wrists under his pillow, and wrapped the leg chain to his belt. It was all he had for a weapon.

He checked the hair across the door. If the hair was ever out of place, he planned to leave and not return.

Every night came the moment. If the door opened and he was discovered, he had no doubt that his options would become even more limited.

He reached the window in two swift strides. Opening the shutters allowed moonlight to flood the room, and he marveled at the difference in the light. A world of indigo and lime went russet at night, or bloody if one wasn't in an upbeat kind of mood. With his decisions made, and some part of him telling him that he'd finally got it right, he was in an upbeat kind of mood.

"I'll be fine," came Arran's voice behind him.

He turned as fast as he'd ever moved in his life, but it was too late. The moonlight outlined Gilead Tan and his free hands and feet, his hair moving in the breeze of the open window, and underscored his ability to climb walls like some kind of insect.

Arran stood expressionless, the door closed behind him. The moonlight showed that much. His eyes were hooded and dark, and the clear lines of his mouth stayed at rest. He studied Gilead and his freedom. Only the slightest motion of the muscles of his young face betrayed a reaction, and what it was, Gilead could not tell. Like prey facing the hunter, he did not move.

One sign from Arran, and Gilead would be out the window. This time, he expected to make it to the ground before Arran could round up a welcoming committee.

"May I?" Arran asked, gesturing to a chair.

"Certainly," Gilead said. He stayed by the window, his own face in shadow. Arran's was clear.

Completely ignoring Gilead's unbound state, Arran sat down. "I have a question for you. It's something I've been thinking about for a while."

"I hope I can help," Gilead said cautiously, more than a little unnerved by the Arran's failure to mention Gilead's missing metal jewelry. The artificial air of civility Arran evoked made him want to sit down, too, cross his legs, converse convivially. It took an act of will not to. This might be a trick to delay him while the guard ran for reinforcements.

"I realized," Arran said, and his voice was distant, as if he spoke more to himself than to Gilead, "that you know some of the sleepers. You know who has what skills. You may even know the backgrounds of some of them."

When he paused, Gilead nodded and said, "That's true." He had no idea where Arran was going with this.

"It struck me, that you could help me choose who to awaken in your place."

Gilead relaxed a little. This might be real. Arran was

a strange one. "What are you looking for?" He wondered whether his answer should be Llew. A combat wake wasn't gentle.

"I was thinking," Arran said, "that I must wake a soldier, as the king desires, but one who also has an interest and background in science. Someone who could teach—as you had planned to."

Gilead's mind raced. If he said Llew, Arran would notice Llew's absence in the morning—assuming Arran didn't have Gilead chained back up when he left. Something told him that wasn't going to happen, but he didn't want to rely on wishful thinking. Stalling, he said, "You want to know if I know anyone like that?"

"Yes."

"Mason was like that," he said bitterly, without thinking, and realized he did it just to cause pain. Going by the look on Arran's face it had worked. McCrary was right— Gilead wasn't a people person.

"Surely he was not the only one," Arran said. He laced his fingers under his chin. He was very white in the moonlight.

Gilead was seldom tongue-tied, seldom slow to make a call. He could decide and implement with the best of them. If he named Llew, his friend would have a safer, gentler awakening. His strength would last, as long as he didn't run around like a maniac like Gilead had. A combat wake delayed the chemical upheaval and flush for days. When it hit, it hit hard, but, coming out of a jump, there was usually time for a full flush. Space was vast. No one would thank him for a combat wake on day three or four, but by that time they might have reached some safety.

But if he told Arran about Llew they might move him, and Gilead wouldn't see him ever, because Gilead would be going down.

As if tiring of Gilead's indecision, Arran said, "I was

thinking of waking this person very soon. You are in no state to go back under, but you could have some time together."

"Is that allowed?" Gilead asked dubiously. He crossed his arms across his chest and settled his shoulders against the wall by the window. It would be good to have Llew's help.

Arran's voice was bland, that of the most callous of young lieutenants. "This hasn't happened before, and I haven't asked."

"Llewellyn Engberg," Gilead heard himself saying. The part of him that made decisions had apparently found Arran's statement sufficient. It would be a cruel sort of trick to come ask Gilead this and then kill Llew. "I knew him at the end of my service," Gilead lied, hoping to sound disinterested and objective. "He was very good with machines, and was studying engineering on his own."

"Could he design a power plant?" Despite the moonlight, despite the neutral expression that Arran maintained with such diligence, his voice betrayed him. The studied casualness was not casual at all.

"Absolutely," Gilead said. "Six of 'em. He could build you a dam."

"Does he have a wife?" Arran asked.

What the hell? Gilead thought. "You don't want to torture someone else?"

"I do not." Arran was very definite.

"He doesn't," Gilead lied again. "There was someone, but she didn't want to leave Earth."

Arran stood. "Thank you for your time." He surveyed Gilead in his insolent pose by the window. "Try not to fall. It would be a black mark on my record."

Gilead made it down the wall in record time. No one

waited to welcome him with sticks and nets, and he headed for the kitchens. He wanted more pemmican. You could last forever on the stuff, and he needed to feed almost two dozen people. God alone knew how badly he wanted to take more. So much depended on how much time he had. Perhaps two days.

The fires were banked, but the boy was awake and drawing pictures in the ash. The squalor of the tableau hit Gilead hard. He understood Arran's desire for the magic of electricity. Nwwwlf was a rich world, and man didn't need to be a squatter on it.

He cut his losses and headed for the stables. There had been a closet with panniers for storage and flasks for water. Everything there was very old, but no one guarded it, and it had the advantage that no one was likely to miss anything from it. He stuffed the panniers full of the flasks. He wanted to wake as many as he could in one night. It was good summer approached.

He loaded himself down with all the panniers he could carry, and ran in the moonlight. The forest was dark, but with the slight spill of moonlight through the rustling trees, and his own good night vision—coupled with his new knowledge of the path—he reached the clearing in less than two hours. Part of the journey was across bare rock, and he hoped that any tracks he left would vanish there. His woodcraft was acceptable, but he suspected the Marss were better on their home ground.

The clearing was quiet when he reached it, and he took stock of his supplies. He filled all the flasks with water and reviewed the food. There was nowhere near enough for a group of people, and he couldn't see the two chickens he'd fetched so far.

The group of people. He couldn't make the call. He'd let Arran get Llew, but after that, he intended to wake Linlea and every soldier he had time for. He'd start at one end and work his way down. There would be no choosing. He knew a few of the soldiers from the colonial training sessions, and would have preferred to look for those he knew, but that wouldn't be efficient. Besides, once one was up, he or she could wake others. He wouldn't be alone for long.

Convincing them they had to get the hell out of there might be harder, but he could do it. He wished he had weapons. He stopped, staring at the stream. He was an idiot. Most sleeping cells for soldiers had a section for kit. A combat wake might require combat, after all. A slow grin spread across his face, but he did not holler like he wanted to.

The next thought was as cold as the water running over his hands. His own kit had held no weapons. If the sleeper's keepers knew of the kits, had they also taken the weapons of those still sleeping?

The run back left him tired, and he pushed himself at the end to work up a genuine sweat. He didn't want it too clear that the fever had broken.

CHAPTER 10

ARRAN LOOKED AT HIS PATIENT. Gilead was Dr. McCrary's patient, but Arran thought of the sleeper as his, too. In the king's eyes, he had charge of both of them. "We can't put him back like this."

Gilead lay on the bed, sleep clouding his eyes, a slight sheen of sweat on his face. Either he had just returned from his nocturnal ramblings, or that was drinking water applied artfully to his skin.

"Sir?" the bewildered guardsman said.

"The shackles have to go. Look what they are doing to his skin. I don't want him put to sleep infected. In fact—" Arran paused, put his hands on his hips, and dropped his head ominously, "we must remember that the sleeping cells may be connected." This was a lie. "I don't want him spreading an infection to the rest of the sleepers."

Robert McCrary stood on the other side of the bed, and his old eyes blinked rapidly several times. He knew what Arran was doing and made no protest. Gilead also watched him. Still, the stupid man didn't trust him.

"But the king's orders," the guardsman said. "He is to be kept chained."

"This room is his chain," Arran said loftily. He felt vaguely queasy. He was neither an actor nor a liar and had to count on his natural stiffness to carry this

off. He wanted the sleepers up. He could not do that
without risk. He hoped Gilead had given him the name
of someone he could trust, for waking Llewellyn was
next on the list for the day. "Look at him. I want him
recovered so I can put him back to sleep soon. I plan
to wake the next one today."

This was news to Robert, who blurted out, "Gilead's
not down."

"Think of how long it took Gilead to learn the sword,"
Arran said. He felt like an idiot saying that: it had taken
blindingly little time for the man to master it. "The
summer campaigns are coming, and we will need him
ready. Also, what if he dies like the first one?" Again,
he counted on the general lack of understanding of the
process. The others had already been dead before they
tried to waken him.

The guard had no answer to his last pointless
question. It had been rhetorical.

"Gilead," he said, "if you are feeling better I will be
asking you to visit the lab this afternoon. I do not want
a repeat of what happened with you. I do not wish
the sleeper to be alarmed, so I would like you there to
explain it."

Robert's eyes bugged out so hard he had to squeeze
them shut to counteract the effect.

"Sir," the guard said dubiously, and then stopped.
He was a young man, and had likely come off some
farm. He gathered his courage and went on. "Do you
think that's wise? This one could get the new sleeper
all riled up."

"So he can't make it any worse," Arran said. "Maybe
the soldiers awaken all riled up. They have to be ready
for battle, after all."

Gilead twitched, but then moaned.

It was a fine line. Arran wanted Gilead better so he
would continue with whatever mysterious activity he

was undertaking, but maximizing his freedom might mean that word would get back to Clarence. Perhaps he shouldn't have mentioned the shackles. Gilead had dealt with them with no difficulty, clearly having found the wires by the hearth. No, he shouldn't have mentioned the shackles.

He turned to the guardsman. "You have a point. Please chain him when you bring him to the lab."

The guardsman looked relieved, then dubious again, but lacked the nerve to protest a second time.

Gilead spent hours trying to figure what game Arran played. There would be two sleepers from the same "batch"—not fifty years apart—awake at once. That had to be some kind of sacrilege to these people. Arran had put himself out there to awaken Gilead's friend. Arran knew Gilead had gotten out of his chains. He had even, perhaps, facilitated that. Did Arran feel sorry for Gilead? Was that why he ignored the missing chains? Did he think Gilead couldn't fit out the window? Arran had seen him scale a wall. Surely, he knew Gilead was planning to escape? But, did Arran guess the extent of Gilead's plans? Damnit, why didn't Arran just talk to him?

Gilead knew why he didn't talk to Arran. Arran was the king's man, the king's cousin. Arran probably wanted a more biddable soldier, better technology, and a salve to his conscience as far as Gilead was concerned. Llew was Arran's equivalent of Gilead's last meal.

Fine. If there was a better interpretation of the younger man's strange actions, and Arran was encouraging Gilead in his real plans, Gilead didn't need to know. If Arran wasn't, he didn't need to talk to Arran and make him realize Gilead's own plans were more outrageous and would take Llew and hopefully others away from this crazy place.

Maybe Arran would want to come with them. He could bring chickens.

He fell asleep on that utilitarian thought, and woke to his door guard carefully pushing his shoulder. It was afternoon, going by the shadows created by his northern window.

The man had three other large men with him, sensibly enough, and they restored Gilead's chains.

He lay there. He was still tired from his outing the night before, and could have used a little more sleep.

"Sir, sir. Lord Arran awaits you."

Gilead nodded and sat up. He was fine.

Perhaps Arran didn't care at all about Gilead's health or whether he would live through another sleep. This could just be a ruse to get Gilead back near the sleeping cell without difficulty. Arran knew Gilead was healthy, and might not want to deal with Gilead fighting for his freedom. He wondered why this had not occurred to him before.

He let his head rock slightly, and looked at them cross-eyed. "I can't get up. The room is moving." He lay back down and pulled the heavy quilt over himself.

"Sir, you must," the guard insisted. "He needs you."

"Let him bring the sleeper here," Gilead suggested. He hated this game. He hoped he was making the right move.

The one guardsman left, leaving the others behind to watch over him. He hoped this was over soon. He had work to do.

Not much later, he heard a rap on the large wooden door. Arran entered, storm-browed and furious. "Leave us," he snapped at the guards.

When they were gone, he turned on Gilead. "What is the matter with you? I need you to explain all this to your friend. He woke for a moment, and is now sleeping naturally."

"That's for real?" Gilead said. He sat up. He didn't need to take this lying down.

"Of course, it is. Next time he wakes he'll be stronger, and might succeed in escaping."

Gilead took the plunge. "And why should I help you? You're going to have me killed, basically."

Arran was shocked. The late afternoon sunlight did not fare well in the room, but the oil lamps threw shadows across Arran's face, making his expressions confusing. They weren't confusing now. "First," he grated, "sleeping is not death. Second, if you haven't figured out I'm not putting you back in there, you aren't even as intelligent as I had stupidly given you credit for."

"I'm not a people person, Arran," Gilead said. "And you weren't being real clear. That's how people lay traps."

"We understood each other," Arran said. "I left you unchained that night you were planning to go out the window—and how you fit, I do not fathom—and I got rid of your chains to give you freedom of movement. What could be more clear?"

"You were lulling me into a false sense of security?" Gilead asked weakly. He tried a smile. Smiles sometimes worked.

Smiles didn't work on Arran. "You were already my prisoner."

"But I could escape." Now, Gilead was just being argumentative to save face.

"Because I left you wires to undo the shackles. Have you no subtlety?"

Gilead breathed a sigh of relief. "Oh, no. None. Damn, I was beginning to think I wasn't very smart. I'm not good with mystery."

Arran's anger was palpable, and now he reminded Gilead more of a certain angry kid who'd joined the service than of a certain young lieutenant. "I should kill you. We don't need your genetic heritage."

Gilead stood up and held out his chained wrists. "Lead on, Lord Arran."

The trip down to the lab was slow, and he spent his time checking all possible hiding places, including recessed doors and alcoves, window embrasures, and the occasional large piece of furniture.

They reached the lab, and Arran palmed the swirly thing on the door. Gilead figured anyone could make it work. It wasn't like the starship builders had set it for Arran's genotype. "Did they have to set that to you?" he asked.

Arran nodded. "It was easily done. There is a password."

The lab's contrast to the shadows of the rest of the keep was strong. Where Stampo was dark and murky, the lab was light and clean, a place a man could think in quiet, without having little bugs and large shadows molesting his consciousness. Gilead felt happier.

McCrary stood by a sleeping cell in the center of the room. The lid was open, but if Llew was in it, he wasn't sitting up.

The guards were still with them. They were large. One carried a stick, and Gilead wore chains. If this was an elaborate trick to get him to the sleeping cell without fighting, and in a condition healthy enough to mollify their consciences that he would "live" sometime later, then he was screwed.

"He's in the cell," Arran said, as if stating the obvious.

Gilead looked at Arran, flicked his eyes toward the guards, and then back to Arran.

The pause was a long one. As it turned out, Arran

used it only to torture Gilead, for he finally asked them to leave.

Gilead drew a breath. He hadn't realized he'd stopped doing that a while ago. "Llew?" he said softly. He walked over to the box and, resting his hands on the edge, looked down at Llewellyn Engberg, formerly of Earth. He wasn't Andrea, and Gilead's eyes smarted. Instead, he was a large blond man with a wide mouth that usually found the world humorous. Now, his face was relaxed and open in unfamiliar repose.

Perhaps Llew would not thank him for bringing him back to this. It was better, however, that he get a clean wake with a full flush. Any others would not be so lucky.

"Llew, it's Gilead. They said you were awake, so quit faking."

Llew's eyes opened languidly, and the wide mouth worked as if he were chewing on something. He sat up, pulling up his knees and letting his elbows rest on them, and looked around. He took in Arran and Robert McCrary, Gilead's loose fitting tunic and breeches, and the shackles and marks on Gilead's wrists, which Gilead made no effort to hide. He had every confidence in his friend's ability to read that all was not as anticipated.

"Listen," Gilead said, and he meant it and emphasized it, meaning *don't speak.* "We aren't on New Mars. The ship got lost and found this place instead. They didn't wake us up for a long time, a really long time, and they usually only wake one of us up once every fifty years."

"You don't look that old," Llew observed.

The man could never be quiet. "For once, just listen, Llew. Do you think you could do that?" Gilead was almost pleading, and the note of desperation got through and Llew's eyes went back to Gilead's wrists.

"They're planning to throw me back into the sleeping

cell," Gilead said. If Arran had deeply mysterious and clever plans, that bit of information getting to Llew should mess Arran up just fine. "I'm not the guy they thought I'd be. So, here you are to replace me. And, you don't have a wife to get you all upset about being awakened without her so that's in your favor, too." The first thing Gilead had done on waking was to ask for Andrea. But he hadn't seen one of his comrades-in-arms chained, with his wrists raw and scabbed and old bruises fading on his face.

The doctor shuffled his feet and cleared his throat, but said nothing. It had been a long time ago when McCrary put them all under, and it wasn't likely he'd remember who was married, or maybe even that the colony charter required a high percentage of married couples. Robert did have the lists in his computer. Idle curiosity could have led him to check. Hell, Arran could have checked. If Arran had checked and discovered Gilead's lie, he'd woken Llew regardless, so Gilead should stop worrying about him. So he told himself.

Llew's face lost its good humor. "I'm your replacement, am I?"

"That's about right," Gilead said.

Llew looked from Arran to the doctor and said, "I'm really the better pick. Gilead was always a little crazy. Don't know if you all noticed that."

Gilead introduced everyone, making sure that Llew understood that Dr. Robert McCrary was from their own time, and Lord Arran McDev wasn't. At the end, before Gilead could share any more reconnaissance data with Llew, Arran put his hand on Gilead's shoulder, and said, "Thank you, Gilead. It would be best to let Llew rest until tomorrow when you may speak again. You need your rest, too, of course."

Gilead had forgotten that, and made sure to look tired before the guards returned. "Sure," he said. "And, listen, Llew, I'll be back tomorrow with more things to talk about."

He went back to his room, happy that Llew had never mentioned Linlea, and praying he understood not to. Arran he couldn't begin to guess about.

Gilead knew he had no time left. With Llew awake, Arran would have to put Gilead down soon. He had to act that night.

Gilead dropped the last few feet from the eastern wall to the ground. He was getting speedy in his descents as he became more and more familiar with his hand and toeholds. He pulled flashlight and socks from the boots he had slung round his neck by their laces. He also pulled the unpeeled, cooked egg he had saved from dinner from the boot and put it in his pocket. If Robert took the eggs seriously, then Gilead did, too. Linlea wouldn't need to know all its travel locations. He would start with Linlea. He'd get them all, but he'd start with her for Llew just to be certain. If things went south on him, and they could, he needed to have awakened Linlea.

He still regretted that he couldn't wake any of the civilians yet, but that would have required the full chemical flush in McCrary's lab since they lacked the combat prep. No, first, he would save who he could, and leave that other moral quagmire for Arran and the doctor to sort out. He would wake Linlea first tonight because with Llew up, he had to get her. He recognized the risks of using his friend's wife as a guinea pig, but it was a risk he would have to take if he wanted the two of them reunited. At least Llew had gotten the gentler wake with a full flush.

He would have taken the risk with Andrea if it could have meant getting her back.

His room on the corner of the eastern arm of the fort looked onto the meadow on its northern side, but its eastern window looked onto the woods that marched up the mountain that the original builders left untouched when they sheared space for Stampo.

The red moon was waning gibbous, and showed plenty of light, more than making up for the absence of the white moon.

Tonight he would be heading, not for the stables or woods, but through the kitchens to the part of the fort that would return him to the catacombs housing the sleeping cells. He hoped no one bothered to guard the cells still. They shouldn't, so long as they didn't suspect his nighttime jaunts. And, if they had suspected those, they would have had him in better chains. He wasn't so they didn't, and he put it out of his mind like he did every night.

The shadows were inky, but the moonlight bright enough for him. He walked softly along the Stampo's outer wall. Here in the southeastern quadrant of the giant cross the fort formed, trees were allowed to grow too close for proper defenses to the walls, and he dodged branches of sharply scented leaves that smelled like sap and soap. The light might be russet, but the air itself was lively with the smell of dark green.

He had taken this path many times in the past few nights. There were no windows placed low enough to be a concern, and only one door, which led into the first floor of the southern wing. The door was unguarded from the outside, and he had not risked it in any previous nights. He had been tempted his first evening, until he had noticed a flicker of light through the little window set into the top half of the door for someone to look out of. If someone could look out, then someone could look in and Gilead had. Inside, two men had played what looked like chess. Now, he just avoided it.

He had never counted on the door, having no interest in walking the inside of the fort sooner than necessary, and made his way around southern end of Stampo. He scaled a much shorter wall in the front, landed in an enclosed herbal garden near the kitchens, a garden that had provided him entry for several nights now, and made his way back through the kitchens and into the rest of the building. He gave a special silent thanks to the kitchen boy, for being so very bad at staying awake, and headed to the central stairs. They were risky, but he counted time on the stairs as shorter than time in the long southern corridor to reach the stairs at its end.

As it was, he exited the central stairs at the first underground level, and raced lightly down the western corridor to the stairs at its end.

He followed them to the bottom and made his way through the deserted halls back to the southern corridor. He had been saving every scrap of power in the flashlight for when he really needed it, and he used it now.

He raced lightly along the southern corridor, and turned into the final hall that led back into the oldest part of the keep, the single corridor housing the sleeper's quarters. It was a hall not mirrored in the floors above. He had gone in a large, spiraling circle. An elevator might have been nice.

He moved silently, and encountered no one.

The names and numbers on the list Robert had allowed him to see over his shoulder placed Linlea next to her husband.

He heard footsteps, and dimmed his light. A sulphurous smudge of light blurred the darkness ahead.

His hands flexed of their own accord, and he told

them to stop it. He had no intention of hurting or killing anyone, and when Arran had freed Gilead of his chains the guards had taken his only weapon from him.

The light rounded a bend and vanished. The interloper had turned into the corridor Gilead sought. He swore. He took advantage of the other's turn to move swiftly, with his own light only partially shrouded. He needed to see his footing, and didn't want to announce his presence with noise. The rush of blood in his body felt loud enough.

He reached the door he wanted, but a strange sight greeted him. The door was cracked, and on the other side the room was fully lit. Someone felt comfortable using the reactor's power. He tucked his flashlight in his belt and peered through the crack. His eyes watered sharply in the light before adjusting.

One awake person stood in the room. He was old and heavy, and his beard grey white, but his shoulders were squared even as he turned with a look of terror on his face. It was McCrary.

Gilead slipped through the door.

"Don't close it," the doctor said quickly. "We don't want to be locked in. Damn, son, you scared the crap out of me."

"And you me," Gilead said. "What are you doing here?"

"Waking Linlea Engberg. Is she Llewellyn's sister?"

Gilead smiled. "Wife."

Robert grunted. "So it wasn't me you were lying to."

Gilead spread his hands. "I don't know what game Arran is playing, but he loves that idiot king, and for all I know he's disobeying him for the king's own good. He wanted someone who could build a power plant. That doesn't suggest he's going to let me go, or that he isn't going to bring the king his highly useful, wifeless sleeper."

Robert rolled his eyes toward the ceiling. It wasn't subtle. "Arran can play both ends against the middle for so long he doesn't know what he wants himself. I didn't tell him I was coming here." He tilted his head. "Why are you here?"

"Same reason you are," Gilead said. "To wake Linlea."

"Then let's get to it. They're friends of yours?" He studied the controls on the sleeping cell. "You want to guard the door?"

"I do, but I want to watch."

"How were you going to do this without me?"

"We're soldiers. We can do a combat wake. And I read all your manuals, but seeing it is better."

Robert held out the bag of saline he carried. "This might be a little more gentle."

"Great. I didn't have access. I was going to do Llew that way until Arran asked me to volunteer someone."

"This wasn't a combat ship. How did you have that wake?" Robert asked.

"Everyone I knew signed for it. We got discounts off the ticket if we were willing to fight on an as-needed basis. The direction we were going—supposed to go—had very little chance of it happening. Andrea felt we were taking advantage." Andrea had always hated cheating.

Linlea's cell was at floor level, and ejected smoothly from its niche. Robert couldn't have pulled anyone at head height out by himself.

A thought occurred to Gilead. "Where are you planning on putting her? Were you going to take her to the lab?"

Robert pressed some buttons, and the lid unlatched. "No. I can't trundle someone up there unseen. I was going to wake her here and hope for the best. The saline drip would give her something of a flush. Where are you taking her?" He set the lid propped on the floor. It didn't hang neatly to the side like it did off the table in the lab.

Gilead had planned to take her up to the clearing with the supplies, and, then, the next night, he and Llew would get the others out. "Out of Stampo, but if you have something better in mind?" Gilead asked hopefully. Maybe, Gilead thought, they could wake two people if things went well with Linlea, and he didn't have to spend the night walking her to his hiding space and getting back before morning.

Robert's grey brows went up and he pursed his lips. "I was just going to keep her in my room. No one comes in there."

Gilead kept an ear cocked to the door, but his eyes on what Robert was doing. "That could work. You're not that far from the lab, and we can get the two of them together." If Linlea was going to stay in the building, he didn't want her separated from Llew. They could both help him tomorrow night with the rest. He didn't mention that part to Robert.

Robert continued pressing buttons, referring once or twice to the checklist in his hand. It was written out in longhand, and Gilead wondered how he had learned to do that. He supposed the old man had had lots of time.

"Why are you doing this?" Gilead asked abruptly.

Lights ran down the edges of the cell, and a clean, antiseptic smell filled the air. Robert pulled a mobile, metal arm, no thicker than his little finger, out of the quarters. Gilead had never noticed that before. Robert settled the drip bag on a hook extending from the arm. "There are hundreds of these in cold storage," he said. He pointed to the end of the hall to what looked like the door of an airlock. Gilead had seen it on his first visit. "The code is 3-2-1. Twice."

"I can remember that," Gilead said, watching

Robert, listening for any noise from the corridor. He could see Linlea, her dark skin, her pale yellow hair, the wide nose and mouth. He felt more emotional than he had seeing Llew, and he'd only known Linlea a year. She had come from a later time than Gilead and his friends. Later than Andrea. But Llew treasured her, and, therefore, so did Gilead.

Robert kept talking as the connections between the quarters and Linlea's skin started falling away. "Usually a ship carries duplicate bags for its sleepers, and then a third again. I've used a few over the years on the sick, but there are plenty." He peered at the controls. "If I were doing this quickly, I'd use this sequence." He faked punching the controls, letting Gilead's focused attention follow. "That's the combat wake."

"Thanks," Gilead said. It was what he remembered. He watched as the color returned to Linlea's face, the face of a woman who didn't know it but was lost in time, waking in a dungeon on a world she didn't request. *Welcome to your new life, Linlea,* Gilead thought acerbically, but the bitter taste was more directed toward himself.

She drew her first shuddering breath.

They watched in silence for a long time.

When Robert spoke again, his voice was very close to a whisper, and Gilead might have had trouble hearing him had he not had the enhancement. "I'm doing this to make up for all the people I've left in here. I'm probably one of the few sleepers who could have pulled it off, and I didn't."

Gilead thought about Robert's drinking, and the escape it had offered the older man.

"I used to have long, elaborate day dreams about sneaking down here, waking them up, moving them out to a normal life. Well, normal for around here. But I knew that one of them would talk. I knew that eventually one of them or something about them would give me away, and that I would be executed. It's a capital crime. There's a story of an engineer who woke another sleeper. They killed him. They made sure I knew that story, and it worked on me."

Any question Gilead could think of sounded like an accusation. He kept quiet.

"I didn't even wake my own wife and hide her somewhere near by. I could have done that. In retrospect, I know I could have gotten away with it. She could have moved into the keep as my assistant, helped me in my work." His voice faded completely, as if he were lost in the vivid imagining of what he didn't have.

"I'm glad you're helping me," Gilead said. "My friends will always be in your debt." He took a deep breath. He couldn't believe he was about to say this. The old physician had put himself in Gilead's hands, sure, but he was capable of a mistake, letting something slip to the wrong person, or just messing up. People did that all the time. But it was one more night, and here he was, trying to recoup all his past mistakes. "I'll be getting the rest of the soldiers tomorrow night—once I make sure Linlea is safe."

Robert looked sad. "You didn't need to tell me. I kind of figured. But thank you."

Gilead spread his hands, and looked away.

"I'm the one who lied to you," Robert said.

Gilead knew what he meant, the false threat against the physician's imaginary family.

"You trust me," Robert went on. "But not Arran. He's not the one who lied to you."

Gilead did not see the point of the observation. "Trust is not just about lying. It's about shared interests. You and I understand each other. Arran is an alien. I look at him and see a human, but he's an alien to me. We are worlds apart, Arran and I."

Robert nodded, as if he understood this strange speech. "It took me several years to get around the cultural differences, the missed cues, the body language being off, all the ways you and I read each other. You don't get the same signals from the people here, and Arran is extra difficult since he doesn't fit in too well with his own folks even."

"What does he want?" Gilead asked.

"He doesn't know," Robert said. "He thinks he wants progress, but he doesn't understand the freedom he needs for that. He thought he loved his king, but he hates all the warlike, jock mentality. He thought he would dislike you, but he doesn't understand why that's not happened. The person Arran confuses the most is himself."

Linlea took a deep and even breath, like a woman about to awaken.

"This is going quickly," Robert said. As if she heard him, she sat up and looked around.

Her yellow hair sprang freely around her head, the tightly curled kinks fighting the gravity without effort. Her brown skin was more pale than Gilead remembered. Gilead squatted down next to her and took her hand. "Gilead?" she said. "What are you doing here? This isn't the ship." She took another shaky breath and blinked hard, as if a wave of drugs had crashed through her. Her grip on his hand was weak.

"Watch the IV," Robert said. "I want all of that in you."

"Where's Llew?" Linlea asked.

Gilead had rehearsed this. He had resolved to tell her the things she would care about the most first. "Llew's fine. He's awake. We have a situation, and you need to pay attention because we're all in danger, including you and Llew."

She fought the drugs with a visible effort. "I'm good." She looked around and noticed she was on the floor. Yellow eyebrows, vivid against the brown skin, rose in surprise. "But we're not?"

"No, we're on a planet we never meant to reach, and it's been settled for centuries now, and they refused to wake us all—particularly the former military."

"That's not very friendly," Linlea said.

The door clicked closed—and locked. Robert and Gilead both swore. He had not heard anyone. His focus on Linlea had distracted him, and now they were trapped.

Robert's face was ashen and his voice shook as he looked at Gilead. "Now what do we do?"

"We wake the rest," Gilead said. "And we start with the soldiers."

He patted his shirt pocket. He only had one egg.

CHAPTER 11

ARRAN WOKE TO THE SOUND of a rider exchanging greetings with the guard at the gate. The rider invoked the king's name, and the gate sounded loud as it opened in the quiet of the night.

Arran's room was set back from the courtyard, but close enough that he could hear the rider demanding to see Lord Arran immediately because the king had questions for Lord Arran. Protests followed. It was well past midnight, and the guard didn't find the idea of waking Lord Arran an attractive one. Arran, who had been well aware that unchaining Gilead might provoke a reaction, although not this soon, got out of bed.

Arran listened to what he could hear of the exchange while he dressed. He pulled on breeches and a thicker pair of stockings. Boots, shirt, the vest with all the pockets, a coat, all followed rapidly. He had a pair of house slippers that likely weren't big enough for Llew, but they would stretch. He stuck one in each lower pocket of the vest. The man's feet would be tender. In the upper pockets he stuck two rolls and a potato he hadn't eaten earlier. He grabbed his largest pair of breeches and an old shirt.

He hoped Gilead had more supplies than what Arran could offer from his pockets, but that would be Gilead's lookout. He could get Llew out of the keep. That he could do. Gilead and Llew would have to find each other on their own.

From the quiet below, he assumed the guard had finally relented, and that they were on their way to awaken him. He left his room and headed for the stairs. Robert's lab was two floors down and, as long as the rider and the guard took the other more likely stairs, he shouldn't meet them on his way down.

He met no one. The only guards posted were outside Gilead's room and at the exits to the outside, and they were just to keep Gilead in. The Pan had never approached from this side of the valley.

The door to Robert's lab was locked to keep Llew from wandering around. Arran swiped his palm across the pad, and entered.

Llew sat at one of the consoles, manipulating the controls as well as Robert did. A large screen full of names was open at one end of the bank, and the other held orbital pictures of Nwwwlf. Llew was flicking through the inset pictures, and Arran recognized the valley of First Landing, and Stampo's surroundings.

The blond head turned, and Llew pointed at the keep. "We're here?"

Arran stifled the urge to tell the sleeper he shouldn't be at the controls, and said, instead, holding out the shirt and breeches he had brought, "Put these on. We have to go, and, yes, that's the keep we're in."

Llew stood up slowly, as if not wanting to startle Arran, and gestured to his own loose fitting clothes. "I'm very comfortable in this." He was looking at Arran as if deciding whether to trust him or not. Arran had seen that look many times on Gilead's face.

"And not well disguised," Arran replied, and he forcibly thrust the clothes into the other's arms. "You have to come with me. Gilead probably will need our help, and you're going to be leaving the keep tonight if we can get you out before the king's men find you."

Llew's eyebrows crawled up his forehead. His mouth

quirked. "The king's men?" he repeated, as if it were humorous. He took the clothes, and started putting on the shirt, but eyed the breeches dubiously.

"They're mine, and they're clean," Arran snapped. "Put them on. It might give us some time if you look normal. And the slippers."

He talked while Llew struggled into his clothes. "I wasn't supposed to wake you. I broke the law in doing so. Gilead is pretending to be sick. I think. I believe he is making preparations for an escape, and I'm going to try to get you out of here so you can join him."

The look of distrust returned. "Fine," Llew said, "but I'm not leaving without my wife."

It caused a pang. Gilead never, ever trusted Arran. He almost blurted it aloud, and then he almost said, "You have a wife?" but the look of distrust would grow. He didn't need the man to have time to think through all of Gilead's underhanded warnings. But it was his own caution that had gotten him to this state of affairs. Maybe this one could be taught to believe him, even if only for a few hours, so he said, "I assume that is what Gilead is doing tonight. He made sure I wouldn't know about your wife."

"He doesn't trust you?"

"No. And I never trusted him. It's made plotting together very difficult."

Llew's mouth quirked again. "I don't understand, but okay." He went to his sleeping cell and pulled a bag from the bottom of it. It was where his clothes had been, and had straps that allowed it to serve as a knapsack. Next, Llew surveyed the remains of his meal. Arran had ordered too large a one for him earlier in the day. Three uneaten hardboiled eggs sat there.

"Take the eggs," Arran said as Llew picked up the rolls.

"They'll break."

"It doesn't matter. Eat one every day. Catch chickens. You'll need them."

Llew made no further protests and took the eggs. He picked up a few more things from around the room, and pulled something out of the wall near the console.

"Come," Arran said impatiently. "They will eventually look for me here."

The dimly lit path in the hall caused Llew no troubles, and reminded Arran that Gilead could see in the dark better than most. Nwwwlf couldn't even keep all its children alive and its women safe through childbirth, but these men had enhancements that still worked after three centuries of sleep. Not for the first time, Arran cursed the ancestors.

The hall was dim, but not quiet. He could hear voices on the floor above, and he led Llew to the stairs. "Don't talk if we meet anyone. You sound just like Gilead."

"That's a terrible thing," Llew agreed. They walked quickly, and Arran consoled himself with thoughts of Gilead's maniacal energy on first awakening. This man had at least had a chance to rest and eat.

They had just reached the stairwell when Arran heard his name called. He stopped and turned. Except for his stomach, which churned, and his heart, which was loud, and his ears, which roared, he felt no fear. His mind was still. He could ignore his body. "Yes?" he said, and was pleased that his voice sounded just the same as it always did.

"Lord Arran," the man said, "this rider, Dawson James, comes from the king. He has questions for you."

Arran blinked like one of his tutors used to, rapidly and stuffily. "Then it's a good thing I'm awake in the middle of the night."

The rider looked like one of the king's knights, tall and athletic, not too large for a fast horse. Arran did not recognize him. "If I may ask, my lord," the rider said, "what are you doing up in the middle of the night?"

"I was moving tanks for Dr. McCrary. He is attempting to create an aseptic solution, but the fluids need changing every four hours." It was arrogance, telling them these things that made no sense, assuming they wouldn't know. They didn't. Arran tilted his head at Llew. "This fellow was helping me. Now, how may I help you?"

"The king heard that you planned to wake another sleeper. Before Gilead went back to his cell."

"Indeed I do," said Arran. "I was worried about having someone ready for the summer campaigns." He watched closely and the other man's face lost some of its suspicion. The king's rider understood the logic of that concern. "The doctor and I have everything ready to start tomorrow. Shall we find you a room for the night? Does the king have other instructions for me?"

Both the guard and the rider fell in at his side, Llew meekly bringing up the rear. Arran had a brief glimpse of his face, and the suppressed amusement made him look quickly away so he wouldn't do anything so inappropriate as smile.

The sense of peace, order, and rightness lasted for all of maybe twenty seconds.

"Lord Arran," came a voice Arran recognized. It was Joey, the young guardsman who had been so dubious about Arran's decisions about Gilead. He was racing down the hall toward them at a trot that wanted to break into a run. Behind him in formal array, swords at their sides, was a contingent of a dozen or so armed men, trotting in unison. It was a sight one saw at parade, not inside a cramped corridor. Arran would have found it vaguely ludicrous if it weren't for the mental paralysis it instilled in him.

Fortunately, some part of him could still function,

and Arran held up a hand to stop his own party. They waited patiently for the trotters to arrive. It was still ludicrous, but it was definitely terrifying. This was the idiot who had no doubt sent a carrier pigeon to the king's ear.

"What has happened?" Arran asked before the youngster could speak.

"The sleeper is not in his quarters, sir. I went to check on him. I had heard nothing from his room for so long—no coughing, no tossing around—nothing, and I worried. I went in, and it looked like he was sleeping. I've checked before, but he was so still. It was his bolster, sir! He made it look like he was still in the bed, and I don't know how long he's been gone."

Feeling a little bad about it, but not enough to stop himself, Arran looked the officious young guard in the eye—the guardsman had gone over his head to the king, after all—and said, "You've lost the sleeper? How did he get past you?"

The guard's face took on a mulish look. "He probably got out the window. Sir. Him not having any chains on him anymore."

"What is this?" the king's rider demanded. "The orders were he was to be kept in chains."

Arran waved a hand as if the king's orders could be rewritten by anyone who knew better than the king. Would that it were so. "His sores were never going to heal. I wanted him better so I could put him down."

Again, the rider understood Arran's reasoning, and a look almost of respect crossed his broad features. "That makes sense."

Arran rounded on the pest again. "Was he really gone? You know you were not supposed to go in there by yourself. He could easily best one such as you." The guardsman looked maybe just under Arran's own age.

Someone in the unit behind the youngster cleared his throat. Loudly. "Permission to speak, sir?"

Arran surveyed the gigantic Etienne, who was trying manfully to look helpful and probably hoped very much to be noticed by the king's rider. Arran could think of no reason to deny him, and said, "Speak."

"Joey showed me the bolster," Etienne said. "I heard him hollering and thought Gilead was on him, but he wasn't there. I believe the lad."

Again, Arran looked with cold eyes on Joey. "Had you fallen asleep? Is that why you went in to check?" Arran wanted desperately to draw attention from the window. If Gilead wound up back there, he would need his exit.

To Arran's surprise, Joey looked at the ground.

Everyone understood the implications, but Etienne, unfortunately, did not share Arran's desire to stall. He wanted to catch the sleeper. "So where would he have gone?"

"Maybe he's left the building," Arran said quickly. "Have you checked the kitchens?"

"I think," said the rider, with all the certainty of the sole person who was paying attention to what needed to be done and had the obvious answer, "that he's gone to wake the other sleepers. It's why the king banished him from the court. And, he clearly knew better than to ask. I don't know why he looked so surprised." He blinked, as if surprised at his own descent into speculative gossip.

"Maybe it was the beating," Arran offered conversationally.

"I think we better check," Etienne said. "I caught him down there once. I think he was looking for his wife."

The king's rider, Dawson, took over. "Lead on. We must stop this. If he isn't there, we'll find him later, but we can't let him even try such a thing."

Arran was horrified, but for different reasons. He did not, however, keep the horror from his voice. "They'll die if he tries that without proper preparation. We must hurry."

Joey gave him a look of withering hatred before racing off, finally free to run at the speed he wanted. The trotting unit kept pace behind him, and the rest followed suit.

The group paused at the turn-off that led into the bowels of the mountain. Arran had forgotten the utter darkness of the catacombs. He did every time. Even Joey had to slow, grabbing a lantern from the main corridor and pausing to adjust the wick to yield a brighter flame.

Arran was not a warrior, but he could run, and run he did, with Joey at his side. The lantern hampered Joey, and Arran took advantage of the beam of light to stay ahead. Llew kept pace right behind him, his face grim, all humor gone in the shadows cast by the bobbing lantern. Arran hoped Joey didn't drop it. He made sure to block Joey just enough to prevent him from getting ahead.

A light showed up ahead. It was a rectangle of sharp brightness that could only be caused by electricity. Gilead had to be in there, waking someone and it was probably Llew's wife. "Sir," Joey gasped. "Let me by. You're blocking me."

Arran didn't know whether the others heard, but Llew swore as if he'd tripped. Arran made as if to get out of Joey's way, and out of the corner of his eye he saw Llew's arm go up as he supposedly fell, and the lantern went flying. It hit the wall, and glass and toadfat shattered in a spray of bright fire and shards. Joey went down, and Llew stopped to help him up. From the sounds behind Arran, Llew wasn't very good at it.

Arran reached the lighted oblong, looked inside and saw Gilead, Robert and a woman who had to be Llew's wife. He slammed the door. "I have them trapped," he called out to the group making their way around Joey and the fire. He hoped Gilead had the brains to figure out what to do next.

Llew reached him first. "What the hell are you doing?" he demanded just loudly enough.

"Keeping them away from your wife," Arran said. "If she has yellow hair."

Llew nodded.

There was no more time for explanations, for the others were on them. The king's rider, who had the last lantern, was beaming approval at Arran. Joey was not.

"They can't get out," Arran told the others. "But we can't get in. We need Robert to open the door."

The rider turned to Joey. "Go get the doctor. Bring more men."

Arran hadn't meant for anyone to make that last suggestion.

CHAPTER 12

"WHERE ARE THE SOLDIERS?" ROBERT asked.

Gilead took a breath, drawing the dank air deeply into his lungs. Mentally, he compared Robert's sleeper list to the positions of the sleeping cells stretching away to the door at the end. "You start with the ones on the floor," he said, pointing. "Here, here, and here. Don't pull 'em out. These folks can handle waking up in tight quarters." Gilead himself turned to the one at waist height in front of him. He checked the number against his mental list, and punched out the sequence for Juno Greenspan to waken, for her neighbors Tory Rowan, and Travis Smith. It would be a hard wake, but they'd be ready to fight. He moved on, pointing at Robert's next one, taking care of his own, slowly working his way toward the door to the supply unit. It was nice to have light to see by.

In less than ten minutes, the sleepers were muttering and sitting up. He heard a babble of familiar accents swearing and complaining that they'd thought they'd put combat wakes behind them. This sucked and bit the big one. Gilead found himself smiling.

In one pause while he waited for a light to turn green, he saw someone standing. She was rummaging for her kit at her feet. "Where's my blaster?" she hollered in outrage.

This led to more cries as the rest discovered their weapons missing, or their kits missing entirely.

It was time. "Quiet," Gilead called in his best parade voice. In the silence they could hear the pounding on the door. Robert kept working, and Gilead punched the next sequence on the cell in front of him.

"Are we being boarded?" someone asked, as if aghast at the absurdity of the possibility.

"No, and quiet. Get dressed while I talk." Once he had all their attention and they were hustling, slightly damp, into their clothes, he said, "We are not being boarded. The ship got lost, and we've landed on a habitable world, but some of us have been sleeping for centuries on this planet. The Marss have control here, and they figured keeping us sleeping was for the greater good."

Groans greeted Gilead's synopsis.

"Any more soldiers, Gilead?" Robert called out.

Gilead closed his eyes. "No," he said, his perusal of the lists done.

"I'm getting my wife, then," Robert said.

"I don't know there'll be time, Robert," Gilead replied. Robert knew as well as Gilead the condition she'd be in if he didn't take his wife to the lab. She wasn't signed for a combat wake. He frowned at the rest of them so that they wouldn't interrupt with questions. He owed Robert big time.

Robert didn't answer but headed for the supply closet. It was his call.

Gilead went on. "The people on the other side of that door have an almost religious conviction that we shouldn't be awake. They will fight us and try to put us back. I have no idea if they'll kill us. I'm sorry about the combat wake, but you can thank me later. Our blasters were taken from our quarters long ago. We have no weapons, and they have swords."

He looked them over. Only one still lay in her quarters. "Linlea," Gilead said, "check on that one."

The rest were almost dressed, and several had their kits slung on their backs.

"As you're ready, line up to either side of the door. These folks don't have real firearms. I've seen muskets, but they're unreliable. They use swords, knives, and pikes. I don't know how many we're up against, but there is another one of us out there, Llewellyn Engberg, who is Linlea Engberg's husband." He gestured to Linlea and saw her wiping tears off her face with her sleeve.

She looked up at him, and there was a break in her voice. "It's Gloria. She's dead." Mason's wife. This was not right. Why did all those other people make it and not these two? His chest felt tight. He swallowed. There had been six of them, riding off into the Milky Way to a life of peace, earned through grueling hardship and danger. Now there were only three, Gilead and the Engbergs.

The rest were watching him. He nodded at them. "Sound off. We need names and don't all know each other. Start with the closest to the door."

When they were done, he called two of the larger men over. "We need shelter for us and tight spaces for the bad guys. Help me build a wall."

They began dragging the casket portions of the sleeping cells over to the door, to stack them perpendicular to the entrance.

"Gilead," Robert called from the other end of the hall. His voice was hoarse, and there was terror in it. "I think I need you," he said, as if he wasn't sure.

Gilead had paid the old man no attention as he worked away at the other end of the hall. Robert had two sleeping cells pulled out on the floor, and they each had a saline drip rigged above them. These two weren't soldiers with a combat wake.

He assumed one was Robert's wife, and, looking in the casket as he passed by, he saw a handsome woman not much older than thirty. She was pale, but looked like she was alive.

He couldn't see the other sleeper until he was up next to her. She was in the last quarters before the supply closet. "Gilead," Robert said, and his voice shook. "She wasn't in the system. Her name was written...." He couldn't go on.

Gilead looked at the casket end. Sure enough, scrawled in longhand was her name. He hadn't known she knew longhand. Seven years and he never knew that about her. He looked at her, her straight nose with the little tilt, her long mouth with its full lips, the swell of her breasts, the curve of her waist. Her hair, raven black, was longer than when they'd gone under. That didn't happen. You weren't dead: your hair and nails didn't grow. There was a wing of white off her right temple, but her face was still very young, just not as young as last he'd seen it.

He fell to his knees next to her casket. Her lips were not the color of rubies as he knew them. They were pale and waxen. He couldn't stop himself. Through the agony in his chest, he leaned forward, threaded his fingers through her hair, and placed his mouth over hers. A rosy flush did not spread across her waxen features.

"Gilead, don't," said Robert, but then was quiet.

Softly, carefully, Gilead moved his hands to her shoulders. They felt so fragile. "Andrea," he whispered. "Andrea, hurry." He sat back on his heels and looked up at Robert. Robert's old eyes were damp, but Gilead's were dry. "Take care of her. Wake her. Please." *Now*, he whispered wordlessly. *Now*. "And your wife," he forced himself to say. "Both of them."

Robert nodded, and Gilead made himself get up, go back to the door, and start planning. "All we've got are the caskets," he said.

"And pipes," Linlea said. She had a pair of thin, flexible tubes it looked like she had unscrewed from the caskets. Others held them.

"They have swords, Linlea." Then he saw what they were doing. The tubes were stretched across the door, held by crouching sleepers at either side. He laughed. "It's a start. I also think we've got some battering rams." He gestured to the caskets, and enthusiastic volunteers sprinted to either side of a pair lined up perpendicular to the door.

She had to live. She had to. Robert was there. He'd take care of Andrea. Robert had to because Andrea had to live. It had taken Linlea an hour. He doubted they had that, and he knew it had been about twenty minutes since the door slammed shut.

"You really can't open it?" he called down to Robert.

Robert looked up from the controls on the bottom of Andrea's casket. Had he been pushing something? "No, only from the outside."

Gilead gestured to the nearest person. "Go check the supply cabinet. See if there's anything useful, like another exit out of here."

The man sprinted off, skirting the sleepers on the floor, stopping only briefly to grab Gloria's kit from the dead woman's casket. There was useful gear in those things, even if the blasters were missing. Gilead felt a pang at the ghoulish gesture, but appreciated the good sense behind it. He'd told them all they were in hostile territory. Anything might be useful if they got out of this trap.

And it was a trap. They faced armed men with swords, and he had a group of combat wakened veterans who were barehanded, unused to unarmed combat, and who would not be doing well in about thirty-six hours. He touched his pocket. He still had his egg. He looked down the corridor. And, he might have his wife again.

Andrea was the cause of his hesitation, he knew. He would be pounding on the door right now, if he weren't waiting for her to wake up like an all too real Snow White, but one on whom a kiss didn't work. He didn't need them bringing reinforcements. And there was the rub.

"Do you think they might be willing to talk?" someone asked. Everyone looked at him. It wasn't a crazy question.

The door opened, and the large man who stood there with a sword drew all eyes.

Gilead took a quick look back at Andrea, but she was still down.

They all stood around, and, when the king's rider tried to engage in conversation, Arran asked for quiet. He said he was listening for the sounds of machinery. "You," he pointed at Llew. "Stand here, near the lock. Tell me what you hear."

Llew looked at him strangely, but kept his demeanor serious. He pressed his ear below the numbered pad of buttons, and listened for many long seconds. "I don't hear anything."

Arran drew him farther from the others, saying in a clear voice that anyone could hear. "I want you to stand here and watch that pad. If the lights on it change, I want you to cry the alarm." He stared at Llew who stared stupidly back.

His back to the others, Arran muttered, "How long does a combat wake take?"

"What?" Llew asked, looking stupid again.

Arran had hoped that he'd been pretending. "That room is full of sleepers, and there are soldiers in it. Like you and Gilead. I hope he has the sense to wake them up. If he does this 'combat wake' how long until the sleepers can function?"

Llew pursed his lips. "You are on our side."

"Yes," Arran hissed. "Answer the damned question."

"About ten minutes," Llew said, watching the pad as if it would light up.

"I'm going to open the door before Joey gets back. We don't need his reinforcements here."

He walked back to the door. He knew how to open it, but he needed to give Gilead time. He also needed to get it done before Joey augmented the force of a dozen men. Not everyone sleeping in those walls was a soldier, and he thought he remembered Robert telling him once that there were only about twenty of them.

"What did you see in there?" Dawson asked when Arran strolled back to the little group.

"He had a woman awake," Arran said.

"Just the one?"

"Yes, that's what I saw. One sleeper." He had no idea how he was going to explain Robert's presence. Robert wasn't a small man, and everyone recognized the well-known sleeper. At that point, Arran's lying would be obvious.

"It will be very bright in there," he offered helpfully.

And still he waited.

When he could bear it no longer and began to worry about Joey's imminent return, he decided he could put it off no longer. "I've been trying to remember," he said slowly.

"What?" Dawson asked.

"The code. You push those numbers to open the door. I have seen the doctor do it many times when he was trying to fix the sleeping quarters. I'm trying to picture the sequence."

"Give it a try," Dawson said. "We may be waiting a while for the old man otherwise."

Etienne pushed forward. "I'll capture the little weasel," he said, and he made sure the king's rider was listening.

Arran punched in the code, and the door made a humming noise. Etienne pulled at it as if that would make it move faster. They faced a bright room filled with people—all dressed alike in the loose but fitted clothes that Gilead still wore at times—and open sleeping cells loosed from the wall.

Gilead Tan himself stood in front of a small crowd and what looked like a floating box. He caught Arran's eyes for a fleeting moment, passed over Llew, who was grinning like a maniac, and settled on Etienne. Gilead's dark hair stood in spikes, and his face was streaked with sweat. His pale eyes blazed, and his smile was a rictus of rage.

"Come on down," Gilead Tan said, in a voice that filled the mountain.

CHAPTER 13

ETIENNE WAS AT THE FRONT, his sword held in two hands as the door swung all the way out into the hallway. "They're awake," Etienne screamed. *So much for parlay*, Gilead thought.

Etienne's elbows rose, and the sword went up. Unfortunately, the grandiose doorsill was too high to catch it, and he roared forward. And went down, his rush caught by the tautly held tubing at ankle height. Undeterred by his misstep, Etienne rolled, keeping hold of his sword.

Gilead had a glimpse of Llew, and the vision filled him with joy. Llew reached from behind the man in front of him, grabbed his wrist, and twisted.

Taken by surprise, the guardsman released his grip and then the sword, into Llew's waiting hand, and Llew used the pommel to tap the man's chin just so, caught him and dropped him.

This made Llew a target for the two who noticed, and they turned on him viciously. The door was too crowded to get through in any event.

Gilead couldn't see Arran, who, if he had any sense, would stay out of it.

Gilead had his own distractions. He had a grip on the empty casket, as did five others.

"On three," Gilead hollered. "One, two, three, charge."

Using the casket as a battering ram, they ran it toward the door and its occupants.

Llew would just have to get the hell out of the way, which he did, and the ram caught two of the keep's men in the chest, hard. The doorway was wide, but Gilead just barely scraped through.

He took a sword from one of the downed men, and got out of the way as the sleepers with the casket pivoted it, the ones in the rear bringing the back of the quarters up parallel to the front and pushing forward as if it were the most unwieldy shield ever created. They dropped it on someone's foot.

"Linlea?" Llew asked over the tumult.

"She's in there," Gilead said. "We're going up hill when we get out of here. I've some supplies. Grab any chickens."

It was all he had time for. Newly captured sword in hand, he used it to whack someone on the back of the head, who didn't take kindly to it and tried to turn and run Gilead through.

Gilead declined the experience, parried the thrust, and slashed the man's sword arm to the bone.

He worked his way back inside the sleepers' hall with difficulty. He could see that Etienne had recovered his feet and had four sleepers blocked from the exit. Etienne had a sword and the sleepers were barehanded, except for Linlea who had a skein of silken rope, obviously saved from her kit, that she twirled like a bolo. Etienne ignored the woman, focusing on the men.

"Etienne, my friend," Gilead called, but the other man did not turn until Gilead was almost on him. He blocked Gilead's strike with two hands on the hilt of his own sword, and the trapped sleepers fled to either side. Gilead was armed, and they weren't, and they knew their job was to get out of the trap.

Robert still tended the two women at the other end.

Gilead knew he couldn't pay attention to that tableau, but it was hard. He thought he saw a flash of black hair and white skin. Maybe Andrea was waking up, but he didn't let himself check.

As it was, Etienne wanted him dead.

The Marss had gotten themselves a new and improved sleeper, and they didn't need the old one running around messing with their tidy system. Also, it was one thing to wax eloquent about the man who had beaten the king's champion and was supposed to be put tidily back to sleep, but how could Etienne miss Gilead all sorrowfully if he wouldn't leave?

Etienne was a powerful man who would have done well serving the king in battle. He was wasted in this keep, and he knew it. If Etienne could prevail against the man who defeated Joshua Calhoun, he would be sure to be taken back to First Landing and all its luxuries. So he swung and swung again, and, once, when he forced an awkward backhanded parry on Gilead, a short blade appeared in his other hand and he slashed at Gilead's face. It was a feint, and the knife found Gilead's ribs instead.

Gilead still moved faster than any man on Nwwwlf, and he pulled back enough to avoid more than a slash, but his blood flowed freely.

He had to see Andrea, and Etienne was in his way.

As if aware of Gilead's moment of inattention, Etienne turned and ran toward Robert, who was crouched next to his patients.

Gilead made himself check toward the doorway even as he ran. A lot of the sleepers had swords now, and it looked like only a few of the guardsmen were still fighting. The man in the king's colors was one.

"Get them out of here, Llew," Gilead called. "I'll be right behind you."

Llew was busy, and only nodded, a fact which barely registered with Gilead, who was running all out now.

Etienne stood over the sleeping quarters housing Andrea.

He looked up as Gilead approached, his large face blank, and said conversationally, "This must be the queen's great, great grandmother. This must be your wife."

His sword pointed at Gilead, Etienne kicked the controls on the end of the casket and all the lights went dead.

Gilead roared.

You couldn't give a man back that which he loved the most and take it away again—not and live. His mind went blank, and it was only muscle memory that kept his sword up as he launched himself at the other man. This time, the edge of Etienne's sword sliced through Gilead's side under his right arm, and Gilead felt the steel scrape against bone.

Robert threw himself at Etienne's knees, wrapping his arms around them tightly but with enough sense that his neck, whether by accident or design, was snugged behind the other man's knees.

Gilead's sword fell from nerveless fingers. Seeing that, Etienne smiled, raised his weapon, and plunged it with a slight twist of his body toward Robert's neck.

Gilead didn't scream this time, but threw himself at Etienne's sword arm, his left hand all he had to stop Etienne, which was why it was Gilead's hand that felt the scorching edge of the blaster beam that hit Etienne.

Etienne went down screaming.

Gilead checked Robert, who was alive but with a large gash across his back that showed far too much of Robert's insides, before he looked back to see Llew. Somehow, Llew's blaster had survived the scavenging, and he must have charged it in Robert's lab.

Much as he hurt for Robert, who lay at his feet in a lot of blood, all his attention was on the dead lights on the sleeping cell. Robert's wife was sitting up. Perhaps he had given her the better saline.

It did no good to stare at the floor. He almost wished that Robert hadn't found Andrea, if it was going to end this way, when Gilead's hopes had revived, when he had envisioned having once again, however briefly, what he wanted.

She might be alive.

He really had to look.

Instead, he looked at Etienne, who lay unconscious or dead, his face a blackened mess.

That was right and proper. Etienne had kicked the controls out of Andrea's sleeping cell and tried to kill Robert. The blaster had been too good for him.

"Gilead," a soft voice said. It was a voice he knew.

He closed his eyes, a sweet warmth flooding him. He opened them again, raised his head, and looked into the blazing blue of Andrea's eyes.

She struggled up, and he was at her side without thinking, snaking his left arm around her and pressing his face into her neck. "You found me," she said. "I knew you would."

"I couldn't find you," Gilead said. "How—" he began, and made himself stop. It was a miracle she was here. Right now, he was happy to accept it and there was no time for asking anything.

She answered anyway. Her words slurred, and her eyes were glassy. "I escaped, and put myself in the cell. They didn't know."

"Shh," Gilead said.

"Gilead," she said, and there was something in her voice and he knew it was about the child.

"Everything can wait, Andrea. All of it."

CHAPTER 14

ARRAN WATCHED AS THE SLEEPERS tied the guardsmen with their own belts and clothes. Several were unconscious already, but they all were by the time they were strapped in. Llew supervised the activity, and stripped them of all their weapons and anything else sharp while they were at it.

Dawson raged. "You coward," he said to Arran. "How can you let them do this?"

Arran laughed. He felt a strange combination of fear and freedom. "Let them? I planned it."

He turned away from the king's rider, and found himself facing Gilead.

The look of rage was gone, replaced by a wild elation that was perhaps premature. His dark hair was still streaked with sweat and now stiff with blood, but he held a woman against his left side, and she clung to his waist. She looked slightly older than Gilead, but only because she had a splash of white in her coal black hair, but definitely older than the young queen she so strongly resembled.

"Thank you, Arran," Gilead said. "We're leaving this kingdom, but I hope you're coming with us?"

They would likely all die.

He hoped Gilead had been stockpiling food on his nocturnal jaunts, but he couldn't see how Gilead could have enough for this many sleepers. The kitchens should have been complaining of the thefts if he had.

There were so many unanswered questions about life outside the kingdom. Were the Pan everywhere? Were there chickens? And, he couldn't imagine this small group, fewer than two dozen, constructing power generators or giving him textbooks on electronics and chemistry.

Arran felt the smile spread slowly across his face. "You bet I am."

"What about the other colonists?" Linlea asked. "Can we wake them, too?"

It was a grim choice, and he looked to Robert hanging barely conscious between two of Gilead's people, and at the doctor's wife who was youthful but feeble. His own wife couldn't stand, but Andrea and God alone knew what had made her retire to a sleeping cell, especially when leaving a child behind.

Arran was paying close attention to everything the sleepers said. "There will be reinforcements soon."

Llew nodded. "It's how he got us some time—he sent someone looking for the doctor. But that guy will be back with more."

Arran sliced the shirt off of a guardsman's back and cut it into strips.

"Especially when he doesn't find the doctor," Gilead agreed. "I don't think it will work. We don't have the numbers to protect them, and look at the two we've got. They can't stand under their own power, and they really can't make a run for it. Which we need to do. We woke all the soldiers marked for a combat wake. We had the list."

"How many more are in there?" someone else asked.

Arran sliced Gilead's shirt and the drying blood that covered it off of Gilead's right arm. He applied a pressure pad, and started bandaging the wound on his side.

"Almost two hundred," Gilead said. He was feeling a little lightheaded, and he wondered how much blood he'd lost. "Too many for us to carry. We have to get going. Take what you can from these guys. We'll need it, because we're going to be in the wilderness, probably for a very long time."

It was a sober group that walked up the dark corridor with the guardsmen's lanterns and Gilead's flashlight. He hoped it had a sun cell for charging outside. It should, but it came from the lab so he didn't know. The sleeper's soldier kits should have all had sun powered lights. He hoped.

When they reached the end of the corridor, Joey and a dozen men waited for them. "I knew it," Joey said triumphantly to the tired looking man whom he had clearly awakened. "I told you they were escaping." He pointed at Arran. "He did it."

"I think Gilead did it," Llew said. "Just for accuracy's sake." He smiled his whimsical smile, the one that, had they known him, would have struck fear into all of Nwwwlf, or at least the people barring his way.

"Now," Llew went on, and Gilead breathed a sigh of relief. He knew this voice. It was a voice that told him he had someone else to help carry the burdens. Perhaps it was even a voice that made swaying and fainting okay. Andrea tightened her arm around his waist, as if she could feel him letting go, and she whispered, "Not yet. Not yet, love."

Llew was talking in that very reasonable voice he could put on. He held his magically acquired blaster in his hand. Gilead felt something akin to love for the man at that moment. "I would really like it if you would all put down your weapons and let us pass. We aren't interested in fighting or hurting you, but we will if we have to."

The squad leader snorted, and drew a knife. He perhaps thought the quarters too close for the longer blade.

Llew sighed. "This is what I'm talking about," he said, and shot the man's hand. Llew was a very good shot, and the man was very close.

Gilead admired Llew's respect for human life.

Again, just a little dizzy, he thought it might be okay to faint, but, again, Andrea squeezed him and said, "You need to hold me up. No passing out for you." He wished his blood would coagulate faster.

In the quiet that followed Llew's shot—before the guardsman started gasping and then screaming—Llew muttered, "We need you to get out of here, Gilead. Be a man."

The laugh hurt.

"I will shoot another one of you," Llew said loudly enough to be heard over the screaming, "if you don't, first, take three steps back," – they did—"and, next, put your swords and knives and all that other sharp stuff you have on the floor."

They did that, too.

One man didn't, attempting a rush at Llew, which almost got the rest of them to change their minds, but Llew shot him in the chest.

The guards continued placing knives, swords, and scabbards in a pile on the floor. "Now, kick it over here."

The starship troopers took the edged weaponry. It sounded like a kitchen.

Llew eyed them dubiously. "I feel like a thief," he said.

"You are not a thief, Llew," Gilead said. "They are agents of a government that took centuries from you and would have kept you separated forever from your wife and friends."

Llew nodded briskly, as if happy with the rationalizing. "Excellent. Now, hand over your jackets, pants and boots. And socks." The original colonists would need to blend in.

This was greeted with protests, but Llew fired again, just over Joey's head, and the undressing began.

The troopers bound the hands and feet of their naked prisoners with some of the less clean clothing. Arran, who had apparently prepared for all eventualities, was dressing Robert's back. Eventually, after everyone had sorted each other out, the group made its way as silently as possible out of the keep.

Gilead set two to watch the rear, two to check ahead at each turn.

The sky was starting to brighten on the other side of the walls, and they moved into the dew-covered grass. Although Arran had once told Gilead he was no woodsman, Arran admonished them all in a whisper not to break branches or leave other signs of their passage. They dimmed their lights, and then decided they didn't need them.

Gilead had Andrea take him to the front of the line as they approached the woods. She smelled like antiseptic and the whiff of a sleeping cell that the former military knew so well. She smelled warm and like the woman he had loved for so very long, and who had finally agreed to marry him right as they mustered out.

Gilead was dizzy and possibly delirious, but he was happy. Once into the woods, he stopped the march. "Listen up, everyone. This is important. If you see a chicken, catch it."

ABOUT THE AUTHOR

Laura Montgomery began reading science fiction when she was thirteen, when the local U.S. Air Force base donated many amazing books to the school she attended in northern Thailand. Laura practices space law in Washington, D.C. She has worked on space tourism and launch safety regulations, which, honestly, are not science fiction. She lives outside Washington with her husband, children and dogs. Laura is on twitter at https://twitter.com/LauraMontgome18.

If you enjoyed this book, please consider leaving a review. It may help someone else find an enjoyable read.

MORE FICTION BY LAURA MONTGOMERY

WAKING LATE BOOKS
Sleeping Duty
Out of the Dell
Like a Continental Soldier

IN THE GROUND BASED UNIVERSE
Far Flung
Erawan
Manx Prize
No Longer A Mystery
The Sky Suspended
Mercenary Calling

Or, check her website at lauramontgomery.com

www.ingramcontent.com/pod-product-compliance
Lightning Source LLC
Chambersburg PA
CBHW030310200626
46816CB00002BA/841